YOL

YORKSHIRE

Edited by Claire Tupholme

First published in Great Britain in 2004 by
YOUNG WRITERS
Remus House,
Coltsfoot Drive,
Peterborough, PE2 9JX
Telephone (01733) 890066

SB ISBN 1 84460 309 1

FOREWORD

This year, Young Writers proudly presents a showcase of the best short stories and creative writing from today's up-and-coming writers.

We set the challenge of writing for one of our four themes - 'General Short Stories', 'Ghost Stories', 'Tales With A Twist' and 'A Day In The Life Of . . .'. The effort and imagination expressed by each individual writer was more than impressive and made selecting entries an enjoyable, yet demanding, task.

What's The Story? Yorkshire is a collection that we feel you are sure to enjoy - featuring the very best young authors of the future. Their hard work and enthusiasm clearly shines within these pages, highlighting the achievement each story represents.

We hope you are as pleased with the final selection as we are and that you will continue to enjoy this special collection for many years to come.

CONTENTS

Faye Hitchen	68
Steph Sargent	69
Maria Haley	70
Serena Panchal	71
Emma Russell	72
Elizabeth Athanasiadi	73

Coleridge Primary School

Nicola Salthouse	74
Arron Wiles	75
Elizabeth Singleton	76
Ashley Bailey	77
Evan Ball	78
Ryan Short	79

Dunswell Primary School

Hannah Dodson	80
Katie Martin	82
Ryan Hewitt	83
Stacey Celik	84
Thomas Benson	85
Laura Miller	86
Jake Stead	88
Josh Clarkson	89
Jonathan Clayden	90
Mark Hostick	92
Becky Lovelock	93
Bobby Taylor	94
Dean Steer	95
Sam Oliver	96

Mill Hill CP School

Katherine McQue	97

Sinnington Primary School

Joseph Price	98
Eloise Davison	99
Jordan Brown	100

Rosalie Sampson	101
James Jeavons	102
Erin Smith	103
Ruby Williams	104
Thomas Booth	105
Edward Bell	106
Stewart Cambridge	107

Sproatley Endowed School

Amy Fisher	108
Aimie Louise Rendle	109
Emma Upfield	110
Emily Gilroy	111
Brogan Taylor	112
Adam Mearns	113
Laura Wood	114
Sarah Barry	115
Ciara Dudley	116
Helena Saul	117

Wharncliffe Side Primary School

Emily Monaghan	118
Rachel Revitt	119
Phil Webster	120
Annabel Groves-Taylor	121
Stephanie Duignan	122
Michael Draycott	123
Holly Swinden	124
Kathryn Dewsnap	125

Willerby Carr Lane Junior School

Amy Leighton	126
Sean Rose	127
Paul Connell	128
Jack Gilson	129
Jordan Rogers	130
Amy Cook	132
Aliss Oxley	133

The Stories

MY ADVENTURE

Suddenly I was woken up by the noise of the removal van pulling up outside my house. It was Saturday the 17th August 1991.

I got out of bed really excited, I got dressed and ran downstairs shouting, 'Hooray today is the day we are moving.'

I had my breakfast then I ran into the garage to see my mum and dad. They were in there starting to load. 'Don't put my skateboard in, that is coming in the car with me,' I said.

When we had loaded the van three hours later, we set off on our big adventure to our new house. I got in the car with my skateboard and my older sister Fiona. It took us half an hour to get to our new house. Our home is called Potter House in Potter's Town.

Whilst my parents were unloading, I went on my skateboard to find my way round. I came to some old land. I decided I would contact the council to see if they would let me build a skate park. They said yes, so we got some local boys and girls together and arranged a meeting. The council organised a builder to come and do the work. Work soon began and with a lot of help we soon had the park up and running. We had a grand opening and we called the park Potter's Ramp.

Daniel Hill

THE MAGIC SLIPPERS

Once upon a time there was a little girl called Francesca. She loved to dance. One day Francesca found some magic slippers. She put them on and she could do anything she wanted. When someone else put them on, they didn't work for them. It seemed the magic slippers only worked on Francesca so she wore them every day.

One day Francesca was going to a party. She didn't know what to wear. She didn't know whether to wear her high heels or magic slippers. She decided to wear her heels and take her slippers with her. At the party she used them a lot and so she won every single game at the party.

After the party Francesca was very tired so she went home to bed.

Francesca Newell (7)
Anston Brook Primary School

THE HIDDEN BEDROOM

We've moved to a creepy house. All the kids at school said it's haunted. (I didn't believe in ghosts until that night.)

I was having a great dream when I was annoyingly interrupted by what seemed like footsteps from the attic. I decided to investigate. I clambered up the woodwormed ladders which squeaked all the way. I reached the wooden hatch. The footsteps seemed to come from the doorway opposite me. I put in the key and turned it. The door was warped and I had to pull on it with my full strength before I slumped down in a heap.

Inside a figure of a girl stared at me, she was semi-transparent and she was floating.
'Who are you?' I asked.
'I've been waiting for you,' she grinned,
'You won't get away, you're mine now!'
I leapt up.
'What do you mean?'
'I'm a ghost, can't you tell?' the ghost asked.

The evil ghost rose trying to get into my body. I felt a great pressure on my head, my mind span around. It felt like I was on a merry-go-round. I fought against the ghost thinking of good thoughts, which was all of my memories. The pressure lessened. The ghost flew off screaming into the bedroom, I slammed the door, locked it with the key and cannoned down the crooked ladder.

I was safe away from the evil ghost, out of the attic, I was ready to tell my mum to nail shut the attic bedroom. The evil bedroom. The hidden bedroom.

Rachel Eastwood (11)
Anston Brook Primary School

STRANDED!

'Jenna, where are you?' I shouted at the top of my voice.

'Here,' she answered scrambling out of the smallish bush by our fire.

'Don't go, we must stick together, I think I've found a way out,' I told her.

'Great.'

We had gone fishing as a family and a violent storm began. Jenna and I got washed up onto an abandoned island. Who knows where Mum and Dad went? We've been searching for a way out since we got here.

'Come on Jenna, I think I've found a way home,' I dragged her to the shore and there lay an old, wooden fishing boat. Jenna and I jumped inside.

With hope brewing inside we set off, we both were lucky because there was a map and a compass there. After hours of rowing, we reached England and Jenna and I could smell the excitement drifting up our nostrils. We were going to see our parents again.

They were overjoyed to see us and so were we, it was like being in Heaven. We both decided we wouldn't want to become *stranded* again!

Samantha Cartledge (11)
Anston Brook Primary School

THE SECRET GARDEN DOOR!

Creak. Timmy looked up from his gardening to see what the strange noise was. *Creak.* There it was again, still nobody was in the garden at that moment. Timmy was determined to find out what was going on.

Bang! Timmy had fallen through a gap in the blackberry bush. As Timmy approached an old vine tree, the creak was becoming clearer, 'Where is the noise coming from?' Timmy asked himself. In the distance he caught a glimpse of something that was clean white. It was a door. In the entrance of the door the vine tree's branches clawed around his legs. He ran back to Mr Smith's tool shed. When he'd found an axe he ran back to the gardens.

After he'd cleared the vine branches away, without hesitating he turned the rusty, brass handle. 'Wow,' he said. The garden before him was beautiful. Just then Timmy saw a figure emerging into the garden.
'Excuse me,' asked Timmy politely, 'is this your garden?'
'No, I don't know whose it is, I just look after it!' said the boy.
'Timmy,' he introduced.
'Cameron, but you can call me Cam,' he answered.
'It's a wonderful garden but how come nobody knows about it?' Timmy asked.
'Because it's secret and I'd like it to stay that way thank you,' replied Cam.
'Would you mind if I helped?' Timmy urged.
'Only if you promise to keep it secret,' Cam said.
From then on they both worked together.

Grace Wolstenholme (11)
Anston Brook Primary School

FORBIDDEN FOREST

'Help!' I shouted, as I ran into the dark forbidden forest. My feet crunching the crispy leaves. I heard a distant murmur. I could now catch a glimpse of a fast emerging shadow. I ran. The shadow now turned into an old greasy man with a dagger in his hand.

'I'll get you,' he screamed.
I stopped running. The ivy gripping onto my legs, the branches clawing at me, tearing my trousers to shreds. The shadow vastly approaching me, I was trapped, nowhere to go, what was I going to do? The old greasy man was now glaring at me raising his dagger into the air.

I moved instantly, the dagger scraped my skin leaving a nasty mark, I started to run again. Suddenly I leapt into a nearby bush as again the dagger took another chunk out of my arm, blood ran down my arm.

As I looked up and scanned the area, I was staring at my bedroom ceiling, lying in my bed. I then heard a scream coming from the dark, forbidden forest saying 'Help me!'

Luke Hartshorn (11)
Anston Brook Primary School

THE GHOST OF LONDON

There was a fierce ghost who lived in old London, his name was old man McCawsky and he ruled London. All of the baby boys who were born were killed very painfully. They were drowned by his slaves, who were humans.

The ghost had huge black eyes which were 7cm. He scared people by the millions, then some young girls tried to stop the horrible beast but they did not succeed and were killed.

Then someone found a child, it had been left in the garbage. It was a boy. He grew up to be really, really strong. His mum was killed because she was caught with the baby boy.

He saw the beast's slave killing her, he saw it through a crack in the ground. He got an army of girls and trained them long and hard. One day he said it was time to fight the beast. The girls were ready to fight. The beast changed his slaves to monsters. The fight had begun.

The girls easily killed the monster, the girls then died because the ghost looked in their eyes. The boy got a stone out and threw it at the ghost. To his amazement, the ghost was sucked into the stone and was dead. London wasn't scared anymore.

Adam Fielder (11)
Anston Brook Primary School

THE BLACK FIGURE

'Night Mum, night Dad.'

Amy walked up the creaky stairs and into her room, Amy switched off her light and started to doze off into a deep sleep. Suddenly the light began to flicker. Tears began to build up in Amy's eyes. She saw a vague shadow at the end of the room. Her heart began to pound like a drum. Amy shouted in a quiet voice, 'Who's there?'
Then Amy's mum came into the room and said, 'What is all the noise for?'
Amy was in two minds to tell her or not but she didn't tell her mum anything.

That next morning Amy walked downstairs and told her mum about the black figure she had seen. Amy's mum just started laughing and said there was no such thing as ghosts or black figures. Amy didn't find this amusing or true. She went to bed that night watching and waiting for the black figure. She stayed awake all night until her eyes couldn't stay open any longer.

By the time Amy got to sleep, it was time to get up again. Amy got up that next morning and went downstairs and got some cereal. Her mum and dad walked downstairs, Amy asked her mum whether she wanted anything to eat and then her dad but they didn't want anything. Amy had another talk with her mum about the black figure and after that day, Amy didn't believe in ghosts or black figures or anything creepy anymore.

Justine Hepworth (11)
Anston Brook Primary School

A NIGHT OUT IN THE WOOD

'Let's go!' shouted Emma, looking at her watch. We were going camping out in the woods for that one night. Eventually we arrived after half an hour travelling in the stuffy car. We pitched up our tent under a large oak tree so that our mum and dad would be able to find us.

Night soon fell upon the summer forest, without doubt it might be haunted. After our supper Emma took off her glasses and I made sure that the door was properly secure, then we snuggled down in our sleeping bags.

It was not long before I woke after hearing a blood-curdling scream outside our tent. I sat bolt upright breathing heavily. Slowly I unzipped the door. Peering into the gloomy wood, I spotted two faint figures approaching us. I noticed that their feet were not even scanning the ground. Without hesitating I scrambled back inside forgetting to close the door. I shook Emma. She slowly opened her eyes, put on her glasses and asked me, 'What's up?'
I replied, 'There are two ghosts outside.'
She was in the middle of a sentence when she paused. She stared outside, I peered out of the corner of my eye, there were two ugly faces sniggering at us. Leaning forward I quickly zipped up the tent.

We hid under the sleeping bags and finally dozed off. At 9am we awoke. We were in the sleeping bags, safe and sound, but was it a dream?

Rachael Fisher (10)
Anston Brook Primary School

ON MY DOORSTEP!

'Yes!' I yelled. The maths test was finally over, I was finally home.

'What are in those boxes?' I asked my dad (Peter).

'Oh, just some old stuff from when I was headmaster, which need throwing out,' he replied.

I peeked into a box and saw that there were pieces of paper, not just any old paper, no, they were old detention notes!

When my dad wasn't looking, I took a great big handful of notes and carried them up to my bedroom. As I entered my room, I placed the notes on my bed, whilst examining them. As I peered properly at the detention notes, I noticed some people's names, people I still knew.

The next day I took about five detention notes to school and told a teacher, that another teacher had told me to give them to him/her. I got people into trouble, but only people I didn't really like.

After a few days of doing this, I was in the cloakroom, getting detention notes, when I heard someone coming. As I hurried around the corner, I bumped into Miss Hickle-Berry, (head teacher).

'What are you doing round here at this time?' Miss Hickle-Berry asked me.

'Nothing, just checking I had my reading card,' I said.

'What do you have under your jumper?'

She had a look and I got a five-week detention myself!

Nicole Moore (10)
Anston Brook Primary School

TOO MANY DAYS IN THE WILD

July 31st
Our third day in Kiwi a-go-go land and I'm already missing my walk in wardrobe . . . and my bed . . . and my jacuzzi. We've pitched up tents in the middle of nowhere in Australia, someone said something about a rainforest. I was only allowed to take four suitcases, a carry-on and my laptop, which I needed for a school assignment.

August 1st
Brrr, the shower is sooo cold. Well, if you could actually call it a shower, it's more like a wall to stand behind and a bucket! Oh yeah, it is a wall and a bucket!

All this walking, climbing trees, it's doing my head in. All the activities seem to involve wearing wellies and slimy creatures so I brought all those stilettos for nothing! And not to mention my Dior dress, I'm so sick of khaki and camouflage. What do they think fifteen-year-old girls wear these days?

August 2nd
Today we walked miles, just to do one of those slimy creature trials and we ended up eating ants and worse, maggots. Of course I didn't join in, my breath freshener ran out! But, on the bright side (there's actually a bright side) after hours of walking, we did come across a respectively clear lake to swim in. What's that? It was a swamp, uh oh that's my Prada bikini ruined.

Argh! Get me out of here! I've had too many days in the wild!

Sophie-Anne Frith (11)
Anston Brook Primary School

THE GHOST IN THE WOODS

The wind whipped past my ears, I ran into the woods, I heard a sound. *What could it be?* I thought. Sweat was gushing down my face. My eyes were watering with fear to see such a terrifying thing. A bloody ghost was stalking me like a cat approaching a mouse.

The sweat on my face turned into blood. My sight turned blurry, the devil ghost turned red in fury because he had missed me.

He chased me out of the woods, when the light hit his face he turned into an old man but would he come again?

Luke Butcher (10)
Anston Brook Primary School

MY DAY AT THE SEASIDE

It was red-hot. I took my T-shirt and ran and dived straight into the sea. I had a good swim to cool off. We stayed there for half an hour, then we went to the arcades and played on the slots. My brother won a football player on the slots and we saved our money and went and bought a size 6 tennis ball. We played football on the beach. I won 6-1. We then went and played back in the arcades while my mum and Gary had a pint of beer.

We walked back on the beach and had another swim, finally we went back to the car, had something to eat, got back into the car and went home.

Luke Birch (10)
Anston Brook Primary School

THE HIDDEN TREASURE

There it was. Straight in front of her eyes. Wishing that it could be hers.

Earlier that day, Lauren had told Grace that there was a hidden artefact in the park that was stolen from the famous Town Hall. People had been working all day - 24/7 to find the object but they weren't successful.

That night, Grace snuck out of the house - a step creaked. Grace was so scared thinking that she would get caught.

As soon as Grace was out of the house, everything went silent. Grace looked around, looking at the moon, which was winking at her. She suddenly quickened her pace, as if a pack of wolves were after her.

Finally she had made it to the park, it was midnight, the owls were tooting, everything was dark.

Suddenly Grace's spade hit something hard. Grace's heart was pounding inside her chest like a drum. Grace began digging madly.

There it was. Straight in front of her eyes, wishing that it could be hers, Grace scraped the dirt off it.

That night, Grace ran home. She took off all her clothes outside because they were so dirty from digging.

The next morning, Grace rushed round to Lauren's, giving her the artefact. Lauren was so pleased that they both rushed to the Town Hall. The staff awarded them with £500 each. They had their name in the paper and were very well-known throughout the country.

What a day they had!

Connie Nicholls (11)
Anston Brook Primary School

SHIVERS

''Help!' Nobody was there to help her, screams echoed round the haunted house. She was never seen again,' shivered Max in a withering tone. He ended the frightening ghost story. Boys at the sleepover had goosebumps spreading on their brown arms.

'That's nothing, wait till you hear my ghost story, it's going to make you wet yourself!' shouted Alfie in a rude voice. Alfie usually boasted about himself. He started the story . . .

'Once there was a strange girl called Myrtle. She thought about ghosts and spirits every minute of the day. Black was her favourite colour. One dark night she heard a strange noise outside. Myrtle had to know what it was. She peeped out of the tiny window but couldn't see. She decided to go and look outside, a dark shadow emerged in the distance.

There before her eyes stood a large man with no head! He was not alone - a black horse was there. The large horse galloped on the spot, then the headless horseman grabbed Myrtle. She screamed. Nobody was there to help her. They galloped away in the dark night.'

Boys at the sleepover shivered and felt their heads.

The next morning a girl went missing . . .

Paige Coulthread (10)
Anston Brook Primary School

A MISSING DOG!

Max was a dog, he loved playing in the back garden as the sun hammered down. If it rained Max would play inside the house and be a nuisance. However, mischievous Max is rather greedy. He loves eating junk food.

Inside Max's house, Max was gobbling down his dinner. Max's owner is called Sarah. She has a bigger brother called Scott and two twin sisters called Lucy and Rachel. The back door slid open. Without hesitating Max ran outside. He didn't realise that it was raining heavily.

'Max, Max where are you?' Sarah shouted.
Sarah saw that Max had squeezed under the fence to their next-door neighbour's garden. Max had been in their garden before. The people were called Mr and Mrs Smith, they loved Max but they were on holiday. The Smith family had a cupboard in the back garden. The door was creaking on its hinge. Max stepped carefully inside it.

Without hesitating, Sarah ran down the side of her house, down her drive and ran up to her neighbour's gate. Luckily it wasn't padlocked. Sarah ran through the garden to where Max was hiding.

He was wet and cold. Max was trembling. Sarah picked him up and cuddled him to her chest. She walked steadily down the drive, opened the front door to her house and grabbed a towel for the bedraggled, sodden dog. Max licked Sarah's face.

'Woof!' Max thanked Sarah.
Sarah knew that Max would never ever run away again.

Sarah Miller (11)
Anston Brook Primary School

THE HAUNTED PARADE

It was one day till the parade but nobody knew that it was going to be haunted. Three years ago farmer Dillon Doily got murdered while he was on the animal float. People believe that he will rise from the dead while others believe that he will just stay dead.

The day finally came. The sky went grey, Lizzie did not think it was a perfect day for a parade. Everybody turned up though and they all gathered round to sing the anthem. Then all the floats started coming along. First it was the ballerina floats. The ghost glared at the ballerinas. He pushed one off the float. She landed into the snow machine.

When the parade had finished, everybody went to a party, it had food and balloons and everything. It was annoying when the lights kept flickering on and off. We could all tell that this was the power of Dillon Doily.

When the party had finished, we walked home on our own. I could feel a light breeze. That was the last we saw of the haunted parade.

Kelly Denton (10)
Barugh Green Primary School

THE GHOST

I was stood there, in the black, gloomy dark when I heard a rustling of the leaves. I looked, slowly it made its way towards me, it was a creature in a black cloak with a hood over its head. I tried to look who it was but I couldn't see. I wanted to run away because I was so scared but it seemed I was glued to the spot. I threw my head into my hands but as I started to run, I heard a high-screaming, gloomy voice, I covered my ears. I jumped on the floor with my ears still covered, it kept on screaming and seemed to go on for hours. My head was spinning.

It eventually stopped, I picked myself up and ran, I kept on running until I was at home, I told my mum but she said what every mum would say, 'Don't be stupid!'

I said to her, 'Why won't you believe me?' but she still didn't. The next night it came back again and did the same. What shall I do?

Oliver Green (10)
Barugh Green Primary School

A GLOOMY DAY AT THE BEACH

The silhouette of a tall lighthouse pierced a steel-grey sky, mottled with dark thunder clouds. Bleak, gloomy houses fringed the shoreline as the seagulls jostled in the attacking wind. The wild waves of the sea crashed against the lonely cliffs. While the breakwater was rotting, the sky was getting even darker than ever. The people living in the houses on the shoreline were very scared because of the terrifying wind. The dark, gloomy beach was very forbidding and unappealing.

I walked slowly on the gritty sand. Suddenly I heard an unfamiliar sound. I stopped immediately and listened. I went to the cliffs to explore and then I heard the sound coming from the rocks. It wasn't anything interesting, it was some sticks rubbing against the rocks.

As I walked away I saw it. It looked like a mound of sand but when I got closer I saw a flicker of light. The glow got brighter and brighter, then when I got even closer I saw a tiny bag. It had a gold drawstring, it also had red and blue patches. I slowly crouched down to investigate. I looked at it for a few minutes, then I couldn't stand looking at it any longer. I gently pulled open the drawstring . . .

. . . as I pulled it back there was a speck of glitter. I put in my hand, pulled out my hand. There was a colossal diamond. It started to vibrate and then started to glow.

One second later the diamond exploded and a rock trail was made.

Lauren Brooks (8)
Barugh Green Primary School

OLD BOB'S STORY

Warning! Speak this story in Barnsley accent.

Where our Christina lives, it's not far off Barnsley market, so nearly every day it's, 'Come on kids, we are off to market. Do you know what our Emma's like? She can't be bothered to get out of bed to go, then on't other hand there's our Courtney up early every morning and she's ready. Thing is our Emma and Courtney are nowt like each other, they allus feyt an argue like cat and dog and they never agree on owt. I bet am only sensible one art er 'em all.

Every time we decide to meet up anywhere they're never on time. Well for a start it'll be our Emma's fault, then I bet it tecks 'em half an hour to get art er house, we 'em feytin.

Ah I forgot to tell yer there's one little favourite art er 'em all, I ant told yer about and I see him all 't time because he's always at our house. His name's Thomas and he's a grandad's boy, I can tell yer that. Funny thing about our Thomas is his allus down't garden tumbling over his own feet and then coming in saying, 'Grandad the invisible man's tripped me up again.''

Sarah Thornton (10)
Barugh Green Primary School

THE DISABLED OLYMPICS

'Hello and welcome to the disabled Olympics 2040. I'm your presenter Crutches Carol, first up we have the plain and simple 10-yard zoom where old athletes zoom as fast as they can on their one and a quarter MPH Formula 1 wheelchairs.

Our line up today is like this: First up we have Electra Slow, in second we have Miss Puncture Wagon Wheel and in third we have Zola Snail.

3 . . . 2 . . . 1 . . . and they're off to a ssluuuuuuugish start. Puncture has taken the lead and is now on fire, quite literally. I think her engine has blown up, but what's this, the explosion has blown up the other two. It's a draw.

Next up is the medication javelin, whoever wins gets their sleeping pills. Our first thrower is Launch Alot Abe. He really likes his sleep.
3 . . . 2 . . . 1 . . . throw. He throws and what's this? He's set a new disabled record! What a wonderful day this is for Great Britain. Next up we have Australian Throwing Pooper, can be break the new record? Yes, yes, he can. That means Throwing Pooper takes the gold.

Our final Olympic event is the beam. First up is Fagio Fernando. In this order, this is what she's doing: First she attempts a backflip, but what's this . . . she's landed on her head and . . . ho golly she's dead. Next up is Lee Falls, he's just got on and he's fallen. I'm hearing his arm's broken. Well this is a really bad day. Goodbye from the disabled Olympics. Remember to watch next time, bye.'

Sam Hurst (8)
Barugh Green Primary School

THE HOUSE I'LL NEVER FORGET

'Can I come please?' Lauren begged.

'No you can't,' Sally bellowed.

'You don't understand, there's a brand new ghost house there and I can't wait to go in it,' Sally begged.

'What's this all about kids? I'm sure we can make a compromise,' their mum said sweetly.

Lauren was nine and Sally was thirteen.

'Right kids Lauren will be going to the fair with you Sally.'

At the fair Lauren got to go in the Ghost House. While she was in, the rest of them went on the Screaming Dead ride. When she was in the Ghost House she was so frightened, she was screaming and the lady in charge of the ride had to stop the ride to get Lauren out. She got off and went to find Sally, but she was not there, in fact nobody was there except an empty funfair, cool breeze and a lot of scary noises.

She ran feeling terrified to the exit, but there was not an exit, it was a graveyard. It was all gloomy and there were huge spiders crawling around. Eventually she found her way home, but when she got home there was no one there and who knows where her family are?

Chelsea Dyson (9)
Barugh Green Primary School

THE BOGGLE AT BOGGLE HOLE

On one slimy, rainy, day, Josh was walking down onto the long beach with his best mate Billy.
Josh asked Billy, 'Where's Alex? I thought he was coming with you.'
Billy replied, 'I know but he went missing last night.'
Just then Joshua saw something out of the corner of his eye . . .

Billy and Joshua hurried to a cave on the side of the cliff. They walked inside and saw blood on the floor. They followed the blood trail into a gloomy part of the cave where they found Alex on the floor unconscious. They were about to pick him up when they heard an ear-piercing roar.

'What was that?' asked Josh.
Something soon answered his question, a 10-foot tall tarantula popped out of the shadows and grabbed Billy by the waist.
'Aargh!' Billy screamed as blood dribbled from his sides.

Just then Alex woke up and straight away he jumped onto the spider's back. The spider was very angry and dropped Billy. Billy fell down onto the floor with a heavy thud.

Josh scrambled to his feet and grabbed Billy and turned him over but he was dead! Josh become much angrier than he ever had before and shouted, 'Here I come Alex!' He jumped onto the spider's back with Alex. There was splashing of blood in every direction.

In the end Josh and Alex were badly injured but the spider was dead!

Joshua Herdman (9)
Barugh Green Primary School

THE SPIRIT IS COMING

The spirit was a person who once lived in Blackpool, but one dark night he decided to have a walk on the beach. Suddenly a man jumped out of the shadows and stabbed him ten times before running off.

On Friday the thirteenth of June my friends and me were walking past Blackpool beach when suddenly we heard this voice saying, 'The spirit is coming, beware!'

Then from out of nowhere a man walked past with a can of beer in his hand and behind him was a very strong gust of wind. *That's the spirit,* I thought. I thought also, that the man in front of the wind, must be the murderer.
Then the gust of wind turned to Amy and said, in a dark tone of voice, 'The spirit is here!'
Oh no! I thought the spirit has mistaken Amy for the murderer. We were doomed!

Madeleine Cooksey (9)
Barugh Green Primary School

A New House Is Better Than An Old House

'Grandad,' I said, 'will I ever see you again? Why are you moving?'
'Because this place is a bit too rough for me and your grandma,' said Grandad in an odd voice.
'Will I still see you?'
'Aye, just ask your mother. It's only a 20-minute walk from your house and there won't be as much noise as there is here because it's in the countryside.'
'Ron,' called Grandma Marge, 'we're nearly ready to go.'
Vicky came over, we both hugged Grandad goodbye, saying, 'See you another time.'
He got into the van and waved goodbye.

Matthew Darlow (10)
Barugh Green Primary School

THE GHOST WHO ALWAYS GOT LOST

One night at Cackle Manor all of the ghosts gathered for a meeting. The chief ghost was called Sir Cacklelot and he was in charge of Cackle Manor.

The meeting was about one particular ghost named Sidry, because he was always getting lost whether it was down corridors, cracks in walls or floors. Whatever, he would always find some way to get lost. The other ghosts had to find a way to stop him as they were fed up of having to find him.
He would just say, 'Oh you found me *hee-hee*. Now I'll go and find somewhere else to hide.'

Sir Cacklelot had an idea that if they all hid then Sidry wouldn't be able to find them. It was just perfect.

The next day before Sidry woke up, all of the ghosts hid in places where Sidry would never find them. Sidry got up at nine-thirty and he couldn't find any of the others.

The ghosts carried on doing this all week and Sidry couldn't find them all week. Eventually he gave up and he shouted, 'Please come out!'

The other ghosts heard Sidry very clearly and they all, including Sir Cacklelot, came out and told Sidry about their plan.
Sidry said to them, 'Well if you had told me, I would have listened to you and stopped hiding.'
'Well, we'll give you once more chance,' they all said, 'but if you hide again you will be eliminated from Cackle Manor. So don't hide again!'

Ellie Lewis (10)
Barugh Green Primary School

CAR CRASH

It was the day I had been waiting for, mi first driving lesson, mi dad's takin' mi. Mam war going crazy, the dog war barking, Shanon war bein' a pain runnin' rand after dog. Dad war waiting for mi at the door, holding the keys. I managed to dart across room and art on door quickly. Dad opened doors on car. I started up engine and we were off.

I crashed into wall and dad said he had to take over. Finally after an hour of tellin' me what to do, he let mi have a spin. I tried to reverse, but it war too hard and I knocked over a plant pot. Dad said we had to call it a day.

As we came in door, we saw that the house was a right dump. Mam war lying on sofa as red as mi top, Shanon had gi' up runnin' rand after dog and dad said he had to take dog for a walk. I had to clean up. It took mi hours to get sorted art.

When Dad came in he said it war spotless and gi' mi a tenner! So today 'as been alreyt.

Laura Todd (10)
Barugh Green Primary School

A GHOST PRESENT

It was midnight. The floorboards creaked and the wolves howled but I slept through all the noise. It was Friday the 13th, bad luck for some people, but not me. It was my birthday. I rushed down corridors and down the stairs until I reached the living room. Sitting on the sofa was my mum and standing next to a pile of presents was my dad.

'Open the small ones,' my dad said smiling.

I opened all of the small presents until only one enormous present was left. I had my fingers crossed behind my back as I started unwrapping the present. I hoped it was a new bike. It wasn't, the box was empty.

My mum smiled strangely. I turned around. It was be a joke, I told myself. I looked inside the box again. It was still empty. Mum and Dad had promised that they would get me a bike. I looked inside again and there was something blue at the bottom of the box. I reached in to get it but it sucked up my body.

My mum and dad started laughing.

Where am I? I wondered. I looked around and I was on a street. I wore ragged clothes and had bare feet. There was a woman who said that I could come in from the cold. The woman went to get a blanket. I turned around. The woman looked familiar, it was Mum! She was holding a knife and it had something red dripping from it. Blood . . . I was dead!

Rebecca Holmes (10)
Barugh Green Primary School

THE GHOST FROM NOWHERE

I couldn't sleep that night. I didn't even feel like sleeping. I decided to read instead of sleep. I turned on my lamp and got out my book and began to read. Not so long after, the clock struck twelve and suddenly my lamp flickered off. *Oh great,* I thought, *now I will have to go to sleep.* Suddenly, out of the blue, there was a massive flash of light and something appeared in the corner of my room and it was glowing!

It couldn't be, it wasn't . . . it was a ghost, floating about one inch off the floor. His hair was just brushing the ceiling and his hands were tied together with chains behind his back. The ghost was draped in a stained, white cloth for a top and a pair of muddy brown trousers.

At first I thought I was dreaming, so I got out of my bed and walked over to the ghost. I tried to touch him but my hand went straight through the ghost.
'Oh get your hand out of me,' he said, 'just because I am a ghost, it doesn't mean I don't have feelings. Anyway, where am I? This doesn't look anything like Japan.'
'You're in my bedroom, in Blackpool,' I told him.
'Oh right, I'd better get going if I want to get to my meeting on time. Sorry if I scared you.' And with that he vanished.

I was left alone in my room. I would never forget that night.

Deborah Hill (10)
Barugh Green Primary School

THE GHOSTLY HOUSE

Tom said, 'I am going to move house today.'
'I will see you in a couple of weeks,' said Josh.

Tom ran home and got his suitcase and then he was off to Oakland Drive. The house was dark and murky, all of the windowpanes had rot and there was slime on the roof.

Tom didn't like the house because he kept having strange dreams when he went to bed. He kept having the same dream over and over again. The dream was about his house and that it was haunted.

On Sunday afternoon Tom was going to the pub to get his Sunday lunch. He went into his drawer to get a T-shirt and he saw a piece of white, crusty parchment. There was a note written in blue ink. 'You have chosen the house of doom', it read. Tom looked startled. He ran downstairs and into the kitchen and his mum and dad were tied up against some chairs, with tape over their mouths. He ran to his mum and dad and untied them.
Mum said, 'We have to escape from the ghost of doom, but how can we get outside because there are ghosts outside the front door!'
Tom butted in and said, 'In my comic book it says that you can kill ghosts with water.'

Tom went upstairs and got his water pistol and filled it up. He went downstairs and opened the front door and there were at least three ghosts. He pulled the trigger of his pistol and they melted.

Casey Wood (10)
Barugh Green Primary School

RUCKSACK

'I'm going.'

'Where?' gasped Mum.

'Off into the night,' I said.

I went upstairs and packed my bag. In went my needs and then I set off into the night.

My eyes are a frosty-blue and my hair is brown. I left home because of my annoying brother. He is a bully too. My brother has blond hair and green eyes. He is 11 and I am 10. He has not got the imagination for an adventure and my dad is not coming. Oh no, he is here, I'd better go.

The forest was very cold and full of animals. I found some nice trees where I could make my resting place for the night. I must have had luck with me because coconuts were at the top of the trees.

At twelve I heard a disturbing noise and then I was approached by a tall man. I ran but I fell and he took me hostage. I was tied on a rusty pole for three days, then my time came. I was scalded by a poker and then the man picked up an electricity pole and swiped my leg off. I dangled from the pole and it wasn't long before I fell to the ground.

Then when the man had gone away my dad burst through the door of the man's shelter and burst into tears at the sight of me. Then we both went home.

Daniel Wright (10)
Barugh Green Primary School

KING BALSAW

'Back you beast, back!' shouted King Balsaw.
King Balsaw is a great dragon slayer, better than anyone, greater than
all the kings but a great dragon ripped off his arm. A high-pitched
scream came from the king and as the blood-drenched sun went down,
the dragon screamed at the army with red and orange flames. The army
turned into ash and dust and faded away.

The dragon grabbed the soldiers and tore them to pieces with his teeth
one by one. Then a great knight, King Balsaw's truest friend, swung his
axe and beheaded the dragon.

Liam Dickinson (10)
Barugh Green Primary School

THRILL AT THE MILL

It was 11.59pm and the moon was going down. There was a strange howl coming from inside the mill. It was loud. Everyone in the village was woken by it and they were terrified.

The graveyard digger, on his way back from work, went to investigate. He went inside the old mill. He looked at the floor. There was a sudden chill. He felt light-headed as he walked down the long corridor.

The howling started up again with a burst of volume. The graveyard digger started to tremble and he climbed the stairs. He went into the room where the howling was coming from. Under a table and some chairs he saw a small, dark creature. It was a puppy!

Grant Ashton (11)
Brough Primary School

HANNAH'S DAY

Hello, my name is Hannah. I work at Moorside Mill. I have a mum, a dad and a brother called John.

I have to be woken up at 5am by the knocker-up. When I wake up with the rest of my family, I wash my face with a cold jug of water. At 5.20am I make myself a packed lunch for work. For breakfast I always have a cup of tea.

After breakfast I walk to the mill. I have to be there at 5.40am. The mill was built in 1875, so it is 15 years old. At work I spin sheep's wool into fine worsted yarn. This is how you make it; first you get some wool and smooth it a couple of times then you twist it till it looks like fine string.

For lunch I have a suet cake and it fills me up until teatime.

School starts at 1pm and finishes at 4.30pm. I always walk home. When I get home we prepare supper, which is sometimes a potato broth with oven cakes. We eat about 6pm.

At 7pm I wash the dishes and do some sewing. I then do some housework for the rest of the evening until at 9pm it is time for bed. I have to get some sleep ready to start another day.

Michael Dickinson (10)
Brough Primary School

IN THE MILL

Ben pushed open the door of the old mill. Spiders' webs hung from the walls. In the moonlight even the old machines looked threatening. The door shut, making him jump. He couldn't explain it, but Ben felt as if someone or something was in the room with him.

Suddenly, one of the machines started and a man appeared out of thin air! He walked towards the machine and poked a long cane at it. The stick got caught in the machine and the man was pulled into it. Then the machine stopped. Ben ran outside. The man was outside as well! Ben noticed that he was slightly transparent. One word came to his mind - ghost. He ran as fast as he could back to his house. He shut the door and got into his bed.

Tom Nash (10)
Brough Primary School

HANNAH'S DAY

Hello, my name is Hannah Thornton and I live at number 29 Gaythorne Row. I am twelve years old and I currently work at Moorside Mill in Bradford as a half-timer. When I finish school I will work full time.

At 5am every morning the knockers-up, who hit the windows with a bamboo cane, wake my house up. We have to get washed with cold water! At 5.10am I have to empty the chamber pot (the chamber pot is the toilet that we used in the night) I empty it into the ash pit. At 5.20am I make the packed meals for dinner and have a cup of tea and then at 5.40am I walk to the mill.

When I arrive at the mill, I have to clean and help set up the machines each time a batch of yarn is spun. Three hours later I get to have my breakfast break. I have suet cakes to eat. Four and a half hours later I finish at the mill, eat my packed lunch (potato pies), I then walk to school.

Whilst I am walking to school, I will tell you some more about the factory. It was built in 1875 and is used for spinning worsted yarn, which is made from wool but made from the long fibres in the wool which makes it very smooth. The mill where my father works, washes, sorts, prepares and combs the raw wool.

Well, I am at school now, so I will see you later.

Jessika Honaker (11)
Brough Primary School

HANNAH'S DAY

Hello my name is Hannah Thornton, I work at Moorside Mill. We are a family of four: me, John my brother, my mother and my father. We live down Gaythorne Row in a one-bedroomed house.

This is my day at the mill.

Every morning at 5am we are woken up by the knockers-up, except on Sundays. Then we get a cold water jug and wash ourselves. At 5.10am I have to empty the chamber pot and at 5.20am I make my packed meal.

When I want to go to the toilet I have to go round the backyard. The toilet is called the ashpit. Some people who are rich have toilets in their houses which are connected to the sewers.

At 5.40am I start to walk to the mill. At the mill my work is to clean machines and to help set them up each time a batch of yarn is spun.

My mother works in a weaving mill, where the yarn is woven into cloth and my father works washing, sorting, preparing and combing the wool. The Moorside was built 15 years ago in 1875 and the mill is used for spinning worsted yarn.

At 8am I go for my break for breakfast. For my breakfast I have suet cake and then I carry on working until 12.30pm when I finish at the mill and have my lunch, which is usually potato pie.

After lunch I head off for school.

Mark Wilson (11)
Brough Primary School

THE ACCIDENT

At night the ghost of Laura Clover roams Moorside Mill. She can hear the horses sleeping. She daren't go over to the stables. Only Hannah knows she's there. Even then she tells herself she's seeing things. Laura knows she isn't forgotten, especially by her parents. They live at number 1 Gaythorne Row. She daren't go for her mother would have a fit as she has just got over the fact that she's died.

She worked in the stables with Norman the shire horse. She was riding on a cold winter day and Norman slipped on the ice and she hit her head and died straight away. She was buried in the ground outside the stables.

Her parents mourned all the time. Her brother slowly died of depression. She was missed by everyone. Her best friend even moved away to London.

I know this because I am Laura Clover. I really wish I could ride Norman again. I wish I could see my mum again. I know she misses me and I feel like walking in the door and eating tea.

At 4am I am forced to hide in my hole amongst the rats. My mother earns my wages and I am no longer alone. A few other people have joined me. None are really enjoyable like Hannah. Hannah is my friend, she still remains. I will remain at the mill until Hannah dies.

Eleanor Findlay (11)
Brough Primary School

THE GHOST OF MOORSIDE MILL

Midnight fell and nothing moved at all in Moorside Mill, until the ghost came to haunt the owner.

'1, 2, 3, 4, 5, 6 . . .' mumbled Jeffrey the owner of the mill, as he counted how many balls of wool had been made.

As the ghost turned on all of the machines, Jeffrey's body jumped out of his skin. He crept out of his office, tiptoed down the dark, spooky corridor and into the workroom. Jeffrey's heart thumped loudly, like a drummer drumming.

His hands started to sweat. Millions of questions ran through his mind. The noise of the machines was getting louder and louder. They started to sound like a stampede.

Then Jeffrey took a deep breath and opened the door . . .

The door suddenly shut, 'Argh!' Jeffrey screamed. His face struck with horror. He quickly ran to the light and turned it one. Everything came to a standstill. Then Jeffrey's heart skipped a few beats. He stumbled over to the door, when unexpectedly the light turned off and the machines starting working vigorously. He screamed again and again. *Bang . . . !*

'Mr Stansworth! Mr Stansworth?' One of his employees had arrived for a hard day at work and was looking for her boss. It was Hannah a small, bright, young girl ready to start work. Little did she know . . .

She ran into the workroom, the light was already on and lying in front of her was Mr Stansworth's body. 'Oh my word!' she panted.

The ghost may have killed Mr Stansworth, but he was still hungry for more . . .

Charis Hawkins (11)
Brough Primary School

HANNAH'S DAY

I'm Hannah Thornton. I am 12 years old. Next year I'll leave school. I live with my family on Gaythorne Row. John is my little brother, he's nine. My mum who's called Annie, works as a worsted weaver and my dad, Tommy, works as a wool sorter. I work at Moorside Mill. At the minute I work as a half-timer and next year I will go full time. There I help to clean the machines and help to set them up. I also do lots of work around the house like polishing the range, cleaning and sewing. I would like to show you what I do every day:

5am - We are woken up by people hitting a bamboo cane on the window. Then I have to get washed in cold water that is freezing in winter!

5.10am - I have to empty the chamber pot from last night, which I really hate to do. I especially hate it in summer because the backyards get very smelly!

5.20am - I make the packed meals for my family and me. Also I have a cup of tea which you could call my sort of breakfast.

5.40am - I start to walk to the mill.

8am - We are allowed to have a break for our breakfast and I have a suet cake which makes me feel like I am full so I don't get hungry until lunch.

12.30pm - I finish my long day at the mill and I eat my potato pie for my lunch.

Kirsty Stephenson (11)
Brough Primary School

THE GHOST OF MOORSIDE MILL

It was a dark, misty, moonlit night at Moorside Mill. It was Friday 13th June and a girl called Hannah was working late at the mill with a few other workers and one she knew quite well called Tim. Hannah and Tim had known each other for six years when Hannah had started working at the mill and were quite close friends. It was very hard work at the mill and everyone was getting sleepy. After about an hour of hard work nearly everyone had left the mill except Tim and Hannah.

Tim went to look at another machine that he had to operate. When he came back he saw that Hannah was operating one of his machines. Tim got really angry because he didn't need a girl to help him with his machine, so he went up behind her and pushed her in the machine. Hannah got caught in the machine and died a painful death and there her body lay, caught in the machine - blood everywhere. Tim looked at what he had done. He got so scared he fled out of the mill.

The next day Hannah was buried in the graveyard next to the mill.

Every day Hannah goes back to the mill on a dark, moonlit night and looks sadly at the place where she died, tears in her eyes and thinks how she could have trusted Tim for all those years.

Rachel Hartley (11)
Brough Primary School

THE GHOST OF MOORSIDE MILL

At Moorside Mill in Bradford there is a ghost. She comes out on cold evenings to hunt Norman Tulal, looking everywhere around the mill to find him. She died because of him! He fell asleep under a combing machine, and she pulled him out but his finger got caught, so he pushed her onto it and sadly she was killed by the sharp points.

As she wanders among the machinery it's all quiet, except for a whistle in the wind on this ghostly night. Suddenly she hears the sound of chains rattling as something enters. She hears the voice of Norman Tulal. She lets out a piercing scream, which wakes the entire town. People come running, she flees as Norman lets slip a wicked laugh and he too flees from the town.

There is no sign of her for three nights, but on the fourth night she returns. She cannot see Norman, so she enters the mill not knowing what ghostly danger she could land herself in. Once inside, she sees him. She grabs a comb off one of the machines and aims it at him. *Poof,* she throws it and hits his chains, right through the loops, he cannot escape. She builds a ghost-proof cage around Norman, she should now rest in peace.

Legend has it that she still roams the mill today. I know this is true because I'm the ghost.

Kate Irvin (11)
Brough Primary School

A DAY IN THE LIFE OF CHEF JAMIE OLIVER

Leave the house at 5am. My wife Jules and children in bed. Drove straight to Billingsgate Market to buy fresh fish for my restaurant in London - skate, salmon and sea bass are on the menu today. Now to order fresh vegetables - aubergines, asparagus, French beans - just pukka!

Driving to the restaurant, fingers tapping on the steering wheel, windows down, radio on loud. I've no time to wait in all this traffic, my patience is at boiling point. Jules phones on the mobile.
'Try to be back for 7pm dear.'
I answer, 'Okay, it's all going pukka.'

Eventually arrive at the restaurant, fans are wanting autographs at the door, quickly sign the books then whiz inside to meet my students and the TV crew.

The kitchen is so cramped with all these people. The temperature is rising, fish sizzling in pans, sauce boiling, flames shooting. I shout as usual, 'Watch that sauce mate, make it pukka, speed up mate, smile for the cameras.' The TV crew want to film close up shots, 'Okay guys chop those vegetables finely, pukka guys, pukka.'

Jules rings on the mobile with problems at home. I've told people not to ring when I'm on TV.

Suddenly one of the students screams, 'Help Chef I've chopped my finger off.'
What next! 'You'll be okay mate, just don't serve it to one of the customers.'

'Come on, come on, pukka, pukka.' I'm going to explode!

Nicole Damms (10)
Charnock Hall Primary School

A DAY IN THE LIFE OF FLORENCE NIGHTINGALE

Hello I'm Florence and you've joined me just as my day begins. My day usually begins early in the morn but five soldiers have been brought in so it's actually midnight. I'm on my way to see them now.

Oh dear, oh dear, oh dear, that is nasty. Two men with bullets through their arms and the rest of them with bullets through their legs.
'I can't count on anything but I'll try,' I whispered to one of my colleagues.'

My next stop is a man with gangrene. A cry of pain came from him just as I walked through the door. The gangrene had spread yet again. 'They'll have to amputate,' I said to another nurse. By now it must be 6am and it is. This hospital is huge. I've only seen a few people and I've been up six hours. The cook should be on her way round with the usual porridge and water. After breakfast I need to visit some soldiers who've been badly burned. Nasty. Everybody's had their dinner; I've been up twelve hours.

Every ward I've been in many people are in agony. Some of the people I've seen are beyond help all I can do is comfort them. It's going dark now, I better light my lamp. That's how I got my name 'the lady with the lamp'.

May Bridges (11)
Charnock Hall Primary School

GILBERT THE GHOST

Did you know that more ghosts are afraid of people? Yes it's true! If you or I saw a ghost we would run in fright, that's exactly what Gilbert the ghost does when he sees people! Gilbert the ghost was as white as a snowdrop. He lives in a haunted house and is so clumsy. He could trip over a blade of grass!

Gilbert was looking cautiously out of the window in case anyone was there. He was looking over his shoulder to see if anyone was following him. But then he heard the doorknob turn . . . He ran when he saw the children coming in. But as he ran he was too busy looking over his shoulder to see if the children were following him so he banged his head on the door frame! 'Oh my aching head,' he cried. He went upstairs for a lie down but tripped and fell flat on his face!

But just then, Gilbert realised that people won't hurt him. So he said, 'Come back, I just want to make friends!'
The children came back and said, 'Is that all you want?'
He said, 'Yes!'
'So, will you be my friends?'
The children said, 'Well . . . OK . . .!'

Therefore, the children visited Gilbert whenever they could!

Abigail Naylor (9)
Charnock Hall Primary School

GILLERY HAZARD AND THE SECRET CHURCH

Hi there, my name is Gillery Hazard, I would like to tell you about myself, and how my life changed in one day. It all began when I was woken by a sound, different to any other I had ever heard before. A part of me wanted to hide in bed, but the curious side of me had to find out where it was coming from. The sound was coming from Creep Side. Before I could blink, I was in that creepy old town, which my mum had told me never to go to. Graffiti scrawled over old shop windows, written in what looked like dried blood (was it my imagination?) Trembling with fear, I felt the touch of bony flesh upon my shoulder. I turned around, my heart racing, and came face to face with . . .

'Wizbocue? Laboomsphere? What are *you* doing here?' (These are two of my oldest friends in the world.) 'You scared me half to death - are you trying to give me a heart attack?'

'We followed you. What are you doing here?' said my wizardry friend, Wizbocue.

'Shh . . .' I said. 'Did you hear that?'

'It's coming from that door,' said Laboomsphere.

It was an undercover passage, which led to a secret church, where we discovered the source of the noise.

'A leprechaun? All this *just* for a *leprechaun?'*

The leprechaun spoke softly, 'I have been trapped here for centuries. You have released the magic and will bring the luck of my people to you.'

This was just the beginning of our adventures together.

But that's another story!

Laura Pearce (10)
Charnock Hall Primary School

AND SHE WAS GONE

For she wanted freedom, to run and roam, she pitied every blade of grass. Maybe she just wanted to fly away. Maybe the same thing every day.

She had no followers or lovers, some say she wished too long, but one day there was a puff of smoke and she was gone. The trees only stand witness. People say she opened her arms and flew away into the clouds. No one knows the story of the lost child. Even her parents don't know because no one loved her.

Victoria Rawson (10)
Charnock Hall Primary School

A MYSTERIOUS MIRROR

It was Monday night, the night before my birthday. I was ready to go to bed. I climbed in and I stayed awake for about an hour or it seemed so. I eventually fell asleep.

I awoke to find a mysterious-looking mirror upon my wall. It was silver and black and it seemed to glare at me. I looked into the mirror to find one pair of deep red eyes which I knew were not mine. Then everything went black except the red eyes of the object which was coming very, very slowly towards me.

Suddenly everything shot up in flames and eventually turned into ashes and crumbled to the floor. The red eyes started to move quicker to the mirror surface. A dark-looking figure came out of the mirror and tried to grab me. There were lots of other figures following it. I was petrified!

Then there was a knock at the door, I quickly looked round the room. Everything was back to normal except for the new mirror which was still on the wall. The door opened and my mum came in and said, 'Happy birthday, are you ready for school?'

Was it a dream, or not? But it is one experience, or dream, I shall never forget.

Sharney Chambers (11)
Charnock Hall Primary School

FANTASY WORLD

Josh Blair was no ordinary boy, he had powers. He could bend metal, read minds, but best of all he could teleport.

One day his powers sucked Josh into another world, a fantasy world, where there were beings like no others. Josh didn't know where he was. His heart was pumping fast, faster than the previous day when he started to sweat in his sleep.

Josh ran as fast as he could but he was faced with a Minotaur, one of fantasy world's most feared beings. The adrenaline through Josh's body was running wild, he had to let his anger out on the Minotaur, so he sucked out his powers. Josh had powers to freeze things, and froze the Minotaur. The Minotaur would never come again. The cave was biting cold so the Minotaur was frozen forever.

Josh ran into a hole, he didn't know that this was the den for a two-headed crocodile. The croc jumped out at Josh and scared him. He teleported from wall to wall and finally landed on the croc's head.

Suddenly a loud *smash!* echoed. It was a long, sharp sword. Josh ran for the sword. He stabbed the croc, it died with seven stabs to the head. Josh destroyed all of the beings then he had to face the boss. It was all of the monsters put together. They all had the wounds that Josh had given them. Josh used all his powers and killed the monster by freezing it.

Jonathan Hird (10)
Charnock Hall Primary School

A DRAGON IN MY CLASSROOM

It was a sunny day and my friends and I were walking to school, when suddenly I saw some windows smashed and found out that it was our classroom.

We rushed up to the classroom to find there was a spiky, green and yellow dragon inside. All of a sudden we heard a scream. It had my friend hanging upside down on thin string like a very thin pencil. We tried to get in but we couldn't. It was hopeless.

Suddenly Robyn said, 'Let's get in by the smashed windows! We all ran around the building and managed to get in through the slimy windows. The dragon was just about to eat our friend Romy, when I found some rope and managed to tie it to the ceiling. With all my strength I swung to reach Romy.

All my friends went to find a teacher, but the teacher Miss Williams had fainted so we poured a bucket of cold water over her to wake her up. Within a couple of seconds she jumped up and the dragon was killed.

The next day in assembly we received an award for doing a good job and to our amazement we all got to go to Disneyland to swim with the dolphins - a dream come true, we had the best time of our lives.

Hollie Faye Macdonald (9)
Charnock Hall Primary School

MEETING THE PARENTS

Miss Henderson just had to ask me to look after the new girl Kim. I thought she was a bit strange, she had dark, eerie eyes that followed you around the room and pale white skin.

At home time she asked me round to meet her family. I walked up the cliff to her dark castle, which, strangely, had black clouds over it. Standing at the door were two 'vampire-looking' people, waiting to eat us . . . oops I mean greet us.

Inside, the high ceilings seemed to move, staring open-mouthed I realised they were spiders! On the walls were animal heads with dark, peering eyes. We went into a room that was dark with no windows only a worn out sofa and a television. We sat down and didn't speak. To break the silence I went to turn on the television, it didn't work. To my right I saw a book, called 'How to Kill Humans'. Kim said it was a joke, I wasn't sure, especially when the whole family came into the room and moved towards me. I smiled nervously but they didn't smile back. I backed away and they moved closer.

Frightened, I screamed and ran from the house. I turned to make sure they weren't following me but the house had disappeared. I ran home but didn't dare tell my mum, she'd make a fuss.

I didn't want to go to school in the morning, I knew Kim would be there. When I got to school she wasn't there and no one had even heard of Kim!

Holly Hague (11)
Charnock Hall Primary School

THE VAMPIRE THAT LIVED NEXT DOOR

When I moved into my new house, the neighbours' house was strange. I went round and rang the bell. *Ding! Ding! Dong!* Nobody answered. I turned round when I heard a voice say, 'Hello.' As I looked behind me I saw a dark, eerie shape. As I looked closer it was a bat! I was so scared at first I ran back home and slammed the door . . .

As I rose the next morning, I heard my mum talking at the door. When I peered over the landing I saw a tall, slim lady with black sunglasses sat on her head. My mum called me to meet Mrs Smith. 'Hello,' she said. 'Hi,' I chirped back.

That night as I lay in bed awake, the breeze blew the curtains. I was scared when I saw the bat in my room. As I looked the bat slowly changed into a boy about my age, which is nine years.
'Please, please don't be afraid, it's so lonely being without other children my age, I'm glad you moved in next door.'
He told me he was only a boy at night. But there's a spellbook in his cellar that can transform him into a normal boy.

The next day we went down into the cellar. The spell worked. It was a secret spell so I can't tell you.

As we arrived at school the teacher said, 'Everyone say hello to Francesca and Billy.'
Billy is my best friend now. We play together all the time.

Francesca Horan-Gregory (9)
Charnock Hall Primary School

THE CREATURES OF THE CORE

One day the Earth shook like a volcano erupting. No one knew what caused the eruption until the boss' weapon shot out of the huge crack in the ground. Four fuzzy, black creatures flew out at an astonishing rate and landed in front of William.

William is the only person the creatures want because he has what the creatures need to rule the Earth. They want the amulet of the core. The amulet of the core is so powerful that only a certain human and carnvitores can use it.

The amulet is made of pure gold in a fancy ring with a light blue diamond right in the middle. William got the amulet on his sixth birthday from his great grandad, he is the certain person who can use it. But the only thing is that William does not know about the amulet.

William was terrified of the carnvitores and suddenly the boss roared like thunder. William's great grandad heard the roar and he ran into William's bedroom, grabbed the amulet off his desk and ran outside where William was.

He held up the amulet and said, 'Is this what you want carnvitores?'
'Yes, that's what we want. The amulet *give it to us now!*'

Great Grandad said the magic spell but he said it wrong and the carnvitores could take anyone into the core with them. They took Great Grandad but as he went he dropped the amulet. So the carnvitores did not get the amulet and William buried it. He never forgot his great grandad.

Harry Levesley (10)
Charnock Hall Primary School

Is Anybody There?

Deep in the centre of York, there is a small, ordinary-looking cottage. If you listen very carefully you might hear faint scratching from within the walls . . .

Let me explain. It was the 15th May 1665. The streets had been struck with a terrible disease called *the plague.* Young and old were dying. Once you had it, death seemed inevitable. Screams of fear filled the air as the stench of burning flesh and rotting corpses spread across the city. People were fleeing in terror as they witnessed blood-red crosses painted on the next victim's door. They knew that once the cross appeared, the occupants would be left to die.

The mother and father stared out of the window at the horrific scenes they had sent their daughter out into each day, to do their errands. Did they feel guilt? Who knows? The selfish parents had done this because they were too frightened to catch the terrible plague themselves.

That night tragedy struck. As the mother was putting her daughter to bed, she noticed red boils, seeping puss. As she kissed her forehead she sensed fever rising. She rushed to tell her husband.

Early morning rose as the little girl awoke. As usual she went to the door to greet her parents, but this time it wouldn't open! She ran to the window but it was bolted shut. Although she called, no one ever replied, no one ever came.

In the distance two figures turned for a last look at their small, ordinary cottage with the big blood-red cross on the door.

Kate Heron (10)
Charnock Hall Primary School

A STORY OF A WIZARD

It was a blustery day at Sillydale on Haddock. The old, feeble wizard was writing a passport to the outer dimension. He wrote his description in his passport.

'I'm a feeble old man. I've got a beard that sticks up. I've got a blue hat with rings around it, a smart blue robe. My staff is disguised as a garden cane.'

The wizards were going to meet in the outer dimension, and he wrote to them.

'Dear wizards,

It has come to my attention that those huggermuggers are hearing us talking on our telly communicators. I think we should wipe the race out. Should we?

Yours truly,
Crawley (Chief Wizard)'

Crawley was not a nice wizard.

The committee meeting was held in the outer dimension on the PP (Pink Planet).

One decade after the start of the meeting suddenly an evil wizard, an ally of Crawley, flew out of the audience and chuckled evilly, nastily and horribly. He said, 'By my spell I make a force field to stop you leaving this room.' Because he thought the wizards would not vote to wipe out the huggermuggers he would keep them there until they did.

'Never!' said the good wizards.

Crawley quickly made a spell that stopped the evil wizard doing the spell, because he wanted to go home for his tea. The other wizards were so nice to him that he decided not to wipe the huggermuggers out.

Paul Strawbridge (8)
Charnock Hall Primary School

A School Trip

One Monday, when we were just about to go home from school and we were standing behind our chairs, Mrs Mitton asked Laura to give out some letters.

The next morning when everyone was sat down at their desks Mrs Mitton said, 'Right, does anyone know what we are doing this week?'
Jordan was the only one who put his hand up and he said, 'We are going on a school trip on Friday.'
'Yes that's right,' said Mrs Mitton. 'This Friday we are going on a trip to Twycross Zoo so you will need a waterproof in case it rains, a packed lunch and a drink in a rucksack and no more than £3 spending money.'

When it reached Friday morning everyone got a partner and we got on the coach. We were off to Twycross Zoo. It was quite a long way and we had to go on the motorway. When we were eventually there we got out of the coach. Still in our twos we went to look at the monkeys first. After that the cheetahs, then the tigers, elephants, giraffes, camels, lions and last of all the snakes and crocodiles. After that we all went on a ride and went to the gift shop. Nearly everyone bought something.

When we were back at school and we'd got everything in our bags we all went home.

Evie Brailsford (8)
Charnock Hall Primary School

MAGIC NUMBERS

I went to a football match but something wasn't right. The football match should have started at 2.30 but it was now 3.30. I went and had a look but the England squad had turned into monsters. I went to tell Sven-Goran Eriksson and his glasses went a bit dodgy. We went to have a look and we saw some magic numbers.

We pulled the old numbers off the players' shirts and stuck the magic numbers on. Suddenly they turned back into normal people. They went on the pitch and they didn't play as good as they should have, so I went to my mum and dad and then Sven-Goran Eriksson came to us and told us there were some empty seats at the front. We went to sit in the seats and the match went very smoothly and England won 2-0.

Sven said, 'Those magic numbers really helped, so next Saturday do you want to come in a Limo and invite some of your friends to spend the day with the England squad?'

We did and had a fantastic time.

Shaun Baldwin (8)
Charnock Hall Primary School

SALLY AND THE MERMAID

It was dusk. Sally Thompson was walking along the shore with her dog Max. She was just about to turn around and go home when she saw a fin. She stopped in her tracks. *'I must be imagining things,'* she said to herself and she trudged home.

The next day something amazing happened. Sally was taking the dog for its evening walk as usual, when what should come out of the sea but a mermaid. Then the mermaid said, 'Don't worry, but I need your help. All of the mer-people are dying because people are throwing rubbish in the water.'
'Then I guess it's up to me to do something,' Sally said.

So then, she put up posters all over the town saying, 'Stop throwing rubbish in the sea, save the mer-people', and then she stood on a box in the middle of the town from 9.00 in the morning till 9.00 at night (not including lunch and coffee breaks) and finally managed to talk the people round to not dropping litter in the sea.

To show her gratitude, the mermaid gave Sally a seashell jewellery box.

When Sally grew up she had children of her own and they loved to hear the story, so they told it to their children and so on. And that's how we get to hear the story today.

Laura Miller (9)
Charnock Hall Primary School

EMMA AND HER DREAM

There once lived a girl called Emma, whose lifelong dream was to be a singer. At school she was thrown out of the choir for having a croaky voice and at high school she was picked on for speaking funny.

By the time she was 16 she gave up singing and started looking for a job. She got work in a hairdresser's and trained really hard. She loved her job and was always singing and smiling and being really nice to everyone. By the time she was 21, Emma had her own flat and had passed her driving test.

One day a letter came saying, 'To all people between 18 and 30 we would like you to come and show us your singing talent'.

When Emma got there she was shaking because there were loads of people there. Emma sang her heart out and made it to the final five. Suddenly her name was called, she looked at a man in the corner of the room, he said, 'You've *won!*' and the prize was to be a pop star for one year and her pop name was Kylie.

Eleanor Ramsden (9)
Charnock Hall Primary School

THE MAGIC MIRROR

Rachel and Gareth were at the funfair in the house of mirrors. They were running about looking in all the mirrors, laughing and giggling at how funny they looked. In some mirrors they were very small, some big, some thin, some fat and in some they just looked strange.

Then suddenly Rachel saw dolphins in her mirror, Gareth rushed over to see. Rachel reached out, she could put her hand through the mirror. They decided to jump through, they counted, '*1, 2, 3, jump!*'

At the other side there was an enormous invisible slide and when they got to the bottom they landed on a dolphin's back. But then the dolphins started to swim, faster and faster they got until they were riding the waves with dolphins, but they were having so much fun that they forgot about getting back. They nearly forgot when Gareth suddenly remembered, so they went ashore to the mirror. They went to walk through the mirror, but they couldn't. It had sealed itself.

'How are we going to get home?' cried Rachel.
Gareth lent against the mirror. They waited and waited and waited when suddenly Gareth fell through the mirror. It had opened because of the sunlight. They decided to jump back through the mirror before it sealed itself again. They counted, '*1, 2, 3, jump!*'

Sarah Lee (10)
Charnock Hall Primary School

A DIARY OF A CAT

I heard a few birds singing and I thought, *I think it's time to get up.* I woke up. I noticed that there was nobody around, so I wailed and moaned until one of my owners got up and let me out for a bit. It was raining, so I ran under the hedge for a little shelter, but I still got wet. I darted to the door and yelped until the door opened. Before my owners could stop me I dashed upstairs and jumped on the bed, leaving muddy footprints everywhere.
'Get off the bed you stupid cat!'

I slunk downstairs to check out my food bowl. Empty as usual! Why can't the pet food people make tins that I can open myself? Imagine ten meals a day, all different flavours . . .

After a snooze in the sunshine it was time for a bite to eat (would my owners eat this muck?) Sitting in the sun, watching the birds fly by is nearly as much fun as batting butterflies in the bushes or chewing grass, and jumping on stray leaves. So much to do, what a busy day - I wonder if it is easier being a *human!*

Hannah Padmore (8)
Charnock Hall Primary School

THE SECRET

Edgar is nine years old, short and skinny with tufts of dusty-red hair. His huge ears stick out like satellite dishes. He looks ordinary, but Edgar has a secret . . . a very strange secret! *Edgar thinks he is an alien!*

There are many reasons why he believes this.

Edgar can never eat without spilling food down his front. Is he just careless or should his mouth be in a different place?

He likes to lie on the sofa buried under piles of cushions. Perhaps he's dreaming of his real home in a deep, dark hole at the edge of the universe.

Sitting still is impossible for Edgar. He wriggles about and sits sideways at the table. Is it possible that he is really an invertebrate?

Edgar builds strange structures from K'nex. They look like towers and Ferris wheels but maybe they're transporters to different dimensions.

For hours Edgar is glued to 'Cartoon Network' watching 'Ed, Edd and Eddy' and 'Dexter's Laboratory'. His mum tells him off for wasting his time but Edgar is really studying the peculiar ways of human beings.

Edgar's mum and her friends often laugh about the strange behaviour of their children - so maybe Edgar is just an ordinary child after all . . . But if that's the case, why is it that when no one's looking, his satellite dish ears rotate, scanning the sky for signals from outer space.

'Just a party trick,' I hear you say, 'He's quite normal!'

. . . Or is he?

David Mayes (9)
Charnock Hall Primary School

THE HORROR OF THE DRAINS

One sunny evening a girl called Mandy wanted to be an explorer. Her mum and dad did not agree with this at all, so Mandy went to her friend's house who also wanted to be an explorer. Her parents didn't agree with her either.

They had their bags packed and managed to escape. Mandy's friend's name was Emma. Emma had a ball that smelt of strawberries.

They both got bored so they played with the ball. Mandy made a grab for the ball but she slipped in a puddle and fell down a drain. Emma sped towards the drain and heard Mandy scream. She untied her rucksack, pulled a torch out and switched it on. She slid herself down a ladder into the drain and saw Mandy. She was OK, just a few bruises were appearing.

The next second they saw a lime-green blob of jelly, at least that's what it looked like. It shook out a leg and it turned out to be a man. He attacked them and the next second they awoke in hospital. A man walked towards them - it was the same man who had attacked them.

They ran out of the hospital all the way to their tree house where they talked about the experience all the time. Then, out of the ordinary, the man came to their tree house. The girls had learnt a few more tricks and killed him. The girls thought they had saved the day but had they?

Romy Risley (9)
Charnock Hall Primary School

HOLD UP

Ching! The shop bell rang as a man with a coat walked in, wearing black. With a quick pull of his hat, a balaclava was whipped down. We only saw his face for a split-second and it wasn't clear. He shot his hand into his coat and flicked out a pocket knife.
'Give me the money! All of it lady! Don't try to fool me!'
He began threatening the shopkeeper and his wife.

I crouched down by the shelf. I was the only customer at the time. The man hadn't noticed me yet, since he was too busy fumbling in his coat pocket. Just as I had crawled out into the aisle, the man whipped out something. A gun!

The man started firing his gun around the room. Drinks and food burst everywhere, as I scrambled to the safety of the stacks of beer cans in crates. I hid there, not daring to look. The man ran past me with the money and ran out of the shop.

There was silence. It seemed like it lasted forever. I stood up, not breathing.
'A-a-are you alright?' the shopkeeper's wife stuttered. 'Come here, child,' she said, after calming down. 'Dial the police and your mum.'
I did what she said and put the phone down. Mum picked me up from the shop. I would not forget that day. None of the people in that shop would. I never will forget and I haven't. It was a living nightmare.

Hannah Brown (10)
Charnock Hall Primary School

THE SPOOKY HOLE

One day, I was walking along in a field, when suddenly I tripped and fell down a big, spooky hole. *Where am I?* I wondered. I thought I had broken something as my ankle hurt. I must have fallen on something as I landed.

Everything was very creepy down the hole and I saw something moving. It was a skeleton bone. It made me shiver and I started to panic. I felt very scared as the skeleton bone moved closer towards me. I didn't know the way out and I kept shouting to try to get someone's attention. I could hear voices above me.
At last, a man shouted down to me, 'Are you alright down there?'
I replied, 'No, I need some help please.'

The man tried to help me by throwing a thick rope down the hole, but I couldn't grab on to it properly, as my hands were too sweaty. I couldn't breathe properly and tried to take deep breaths to calm down. Eventually, I struggled to grasp the rope and pulled myself up, just as the skeleton bone moved towards me. I gave a big sigh of relief.

Ben Whittington (8)
Charnock Hall Primary School

A MYSTERY

One misty morning, I was just waking up, when everything shook. *Whatever is that?* I thought. It must be a *hurricane!* Yes, but sure enough, coming towards me, was a luminous green spaceship, with one man waving frantically, shouting, 'Come inside!'
So, with a struggle, I joined him and we immediately went down, down, down.

The wind blew us straight down to something hard. I jumped out of the ship quickly and saw a great number of people rushing in different directions. They looked at me funny, I must have looked strange to them.

There were things with wheels on, with people sat inside. Lots of people were licking the floor. I thought, *what on earth are they doing?* I realised it must be something tasty. I tried it and liked it. Must be made of chocolate.

I was glad I had come here, I didn't want to go back again. It seemed a nice place to be. Everything was made of chocolate and even the people looked brown. The only thing that the shops sold, was chocolate. I couldn't believe it, here I was to stay. No more to be in the clouds, so I'm glad there was a hurricane up there. Hooray!

Kerry Whittington (11)
Charnock Hall Primary School

THE GHOST IN OUR COMPUTER

We were all sitting by the school computer trying to write a story, when suddenly a rather strange message appeared on the screen. It read, *I shall get my own back on you terrible children.* We felt rather scared. We ignored the message and carried on with the story. After writing a couple more words, there was a flash of light and a figure of a rather strange sort appeared.

We told the teacher about the ghost but she didn't believe us, she thought it was all a joke. The teacher turned around to see if she could see a ghost but she couldn't. Miss Hopkinson said, 'Don't lie to me children, otherwise there will be big trouble.' As she turned back to speak to the children, the ghost was standing behind her. We didn't go and tell Miss Hopkinson because we were afraid we were going to get done.

She came across to speak to us when the ghost appeared behind her. We screamed and said, 'The ghost is behind you Miss!' She turned around and the ghost had completely disappeared. We couldn't even see it so she had no chance at all. The ghost had returned to the computer.

Katie Hanson (10)
Charnock Hall Primary School

A DAY IN THE LIFE OF A POP STAR

Today it's a change. It's my day in the life of a singer, but which singer could I be - Geri Halliwell or even Victoria Beckham? But I think I should be Rachel from S Club. So here I go!

I had to get up really early and get dressed. I got up before the boys because it takes longer for us girls to put make-up on. We were finally dressed and had to drive to the studio to record a song - *Reach For The Stars*. Everybody sang their heart out till they were out of breath. So we went out to get a bite to eat. It was not lunchtime, but we were starving.

We got back to find we had to do dancing, so we waited for our dancing teacher to come. After a while of waiting we found out she was ill. I was glad to find out because I was getting worried. Anyway, I decided to go shopping because I love going shopping and I always come out with lots of bags. I did! I came back with three bags.

I met up with the rest of the gang at the studio, but we had a surprise because we found a woman waiting there. The woman turned and said, 'Oh hi, I am your new dancing teacher so let's start.' We were dancing for ages, so I decided to have an early night in.

So that's what it's like for a star.

Faye Hitchen (10)
Charnock Hall Primary School

THE HIPPO AND THE MOUSE

One day in the jungle there lived a mouse. Mouse went for a jog through the jungle. On the way he met his friend. Mouse asked Hippo if he wanted to go for a jog.
Hippo said, 'Yes.'

While they were jogging, Hippo fell behind.
Mouse said repeatedly, 'Catch up Hippo you're falling behind.'
Hippo said, 'No you twig, I ain't your friend anymore.'

The next day little Mouse went for a jog and saw Hippo rolling around in the mud. Hippo tried to apologise but Mouse wasn't his friend anymore.

Steph Sargent (10)
Charnock Hall Primary School

A RABBIT'S TALE

It was a peaceful life, not showered in riches, but humble. I made a living scrounging from the farmer's vegetable patch and let me tall ya that's some good eatin'! As you've probably guessed I'm not human, being as you humans turn down the créme de la créme of veg. Believe me I've learnt from experience as you'll soon find. No, I'm a rabbit and proud of it but it does have its disadvantages . . .

Yes I was captured, but not just by anyone, no, by one of the most selfish, spoilt, overindulged little girls that ever walked this Earth. Her name was Fran and she would tickle me, torment me and dress me in dolls' clothing. But Millie, Fran's neighbour, was loving and kind. Every morning she would slip some food and water into my empty bowls, each time giving me an affectionate pat in pity of how I'd been treated.

Fran's cruelty continued until one night I escaped under the fence to Millie's where, to my horror, there were two Alsatians waiting at the other end, snapping and barking at me. But to my relief they were tied to a pole. The barking disturbed Millie and once again she came to my rescue.

The following day she reported Fran to the RSPCA and they've put her on a course called, 'You and your pet - how to take better care of animals'.

Meanwhile, Millie and me have moved to a farm and so I'm back where I started!

Maria Haley (10)
Charnock Hall Primary School

DAVID BECKHAM

One hot, sunny day, David Beckham went to have his hair cut at 'House Of Style'. When he walked in he asked for red highlights on each side, but he really wanted to be bald all over.

The hairdresser got started. Three hours later the highlights weren't red - they were pink. Beckham loved it but he thought that if Posh didn't like it then she would be mad.

When he got home he showed Posh. She loved it.
She said, 'But you've got a match tomorrow.'

The match was England Vs Turkey. David was scared that everyone would laugh at him, but to his surprise everyone loved it.

The next day David and Posh went shopping. David noticed that almost all the boys had pink highlights. The hairstyle became popular and the 'House Of Style' was famous.

Serena Panchal (9)
Charnock Hall Primary School

A DAY IN THE LIFE OF A VET

It's Monday morning, it's 6.30am and the sun is just rising. Another day of exciting adventures with the animals at the vet's surgery. Breakfast over and it's time for my journey to work.

On arriving at the surgery I am greeted by Mrs Jones and her dog, Bessingham Bramble, who needs to be examined because she is having pups.
'Good morning Mrs Jones, how is Bess?'
'Not too good today, she is not eating.'
'I'll take a look at her, come through.'

Just as Bess came into the surgery she began to deliver her pups. First one, then two . . . she had seven puppies in total and all were fine. What a wonderful start to the day.

Next were my visits to the local farms to check on the cows and sheep. My visit to Mr Ward's farm to see his horse was something new as he had only just got him. Tony the horse stood at 12 hands high and looked amazing.

Just as I was leaving my mobile phone rang. It was the surgery asking me to do an urgent visit to the local park where the police had found a swan tangled in some fishing line. Between us we were able to save the swan and make sure its injuries were treated.

Back at the surgery that day I looked at everything that had happened and realised that two days in a vet's life are never the same and it is very rewarding work.

Emma Russell (10)
Charnock Hall Primary School

A BOY'S ADVENTURE

An orphan boy found his first friend in an alley. It was a stray dog, all alone. The boy, who was trying to get to Jamaica, strolled along the road and into a wood.

After a while they saw a dragon hovering above their heads. The dragon's name was Dragonite.
'Would you like a ride?' asked Dragonite.
'Yes please, will you take us to Jamaica?' replied the boy.

The boy and the dog scrambled onto the dragon's back. The dragon rose high into the sky. She flew out of the woods and over a volcano. The boy slipped. Luckily he caught hold of the rocks and hung on. There was a splutter and a gurgle and a lava monster rose from the centre of the volcano. The creature gently picked up the boy and carefully lifted him to safety. The boy told the creature they were trying to get to Jamaica and asked if he would like to come too. The monster magically transformed into an eagle. They flew off together over mountains and oceans until they reached Jamaica.

The boy said, 'Are you thinking what I'm thinking? Let's have a beach party.'
They congaed on the sand in the brightness of the sun until the sun set.

Elizabeth Athanasiadi (9)
Charnock Hall Primary School

THE HAUNTED HOUSE ON HAUNTED HILL

One foggy night there were 3 women and 4 men. They all agreed to stay for one night at the haunted house on Haunted Hill. If they stayed there for one night they would receive £1,000 each.

On the very night they got there they went into the house and all got scared and shivered.
The person who set the bet said, 'Here, you can all take a gun each.'
They all took a gun and went to their bedrooms. They all heard a noise so they went downstairs and nothing was there, so they went back upstairs.

After a while all of the people heard one of the women scream. They asked what was wrong. The woman screamed because there was a head in a jewellery box.

They all stayed awake until late.
The man who set the bet said, 'At 12 o'clock that's when the ghost and others come out.'
They all got their guns ready at 11.59pm for the ghost. They saw a shadow and shot the shadow, but it was a mouse and they killed it. Then they all saw a vampire and shot it and the vampire died. The later the night got, the more spooky it got. They saw a vampire, bat, skeleton and Frankenstein. They shot them all but the monsters just kept on walking.

It was morning, the monsters all disappeared. They got out, got their money and took off. The council eventually knocked the house down and the monsters weren't seen again.

Nicola Salthouse (11)
Coleridge Primary School

JEEPERS CREEPERS

In 1994 I was on my way home from holiday. A rusty truck came shooting off the side of the road and started ramming me all over the road. I read the number plate and it said DAED. Then I spelt it backwards, it said DEAD. A moment later, the truck left me and drove up the road to a nearby church with patched up windows. There were ravens and crows screeching outside. I glanced sideways and saw the man from the truck dropping bodies down a chute to the church cellar.

At that moment I was scared. I decided to investigate so I started hanging down the chute but I couldn't see anything until a rat made me jump. I fell down the chute into the cellar.

First thing I saw was a body bag. I ripped it open and there in front of my face was a body with its head chopped in half.

I carried on walking . . . I heard creepy footsteps coming towards me, then a zombie K9 dog with a scar down its left eye came screaming towards me. I dived left in horror and fell down loads of stairs.

I was laid out for roughly thirty minutes. I woke up and tried to remember where I was. I made my way to the outside of the church. I ran to my car and drove off. Would I ever escape this horror?

Arron Wiles (11)
Coleridge Primary School

A DAY IN THE LIFE OF BLADE THE KITTEN

We interviewed Blade the kitten of 49 Crown Street. We asked him a few questions about how a normal day in his life goes. We asked him whether he slept in the day or at night.

He replied, 'I sleep in the night but I have naps in the day as I'm only a kitten.'

'I said, 'Please can you tell me when it's your birthday and what a normal day is like?'

He again replied, 'Yes my birthday is May 1st and this is my day.

My day starts at 7am when I wake up from a good sleep and start playing with my many toys until 7.30am, when the house becomes alive. The humans I lodge with make me some food then I tuck in. Then the 3 girls I live with give me a hug before they go to school. Then I play and eat and nap and get stroked by 2 big humans.

Then at 3.15pm the girls come back and play with me until it's time for them to have their tea. I play with my toys, unless I go on the table, which is when I get shut in the front room.

After they've had their tea they give me a quick stroke, then disappear upstairs. Then I have a giddy half-hour where I run around like crazy until they come downstairs for supper and I get a good stroke then I go to bed.'

Elizabeth Singleton (10)
Coleridge Primary School

HOUSE OF DOOM

Ashley was on his way to Antarctica to search for a rare bird, the Ornacthirese, with his companions Arron, Sean and Kyle.

'Come on Sean take this beauty down,' shouted Ashley.
'Okay, but I'll need Kyle's help,' yelled Sean and slowly but surely Kyle and Sean brought the helicopter down.

Ashley was the leader and was rather skinny, but Sean and Arron were quite the opposite. Kyle was the shy one but he was the fattest.

'Ashley look!' screamed Arron.
They all looked . . . their eyes widened.
They saw a graveyard - a massive one at that. Then Arron tried to booby trap zombies when they rose from their graves. They ran to a spooky church and slammed the doors shut. They all gave a sigh of relief but weren't out of danger yet. They all turned . . . there was a hideous troop of skeletons with swords raised and surging forward.

They heard a *bang, bang, bang* on the church doors then *crack!* A zombie's hand was poking out of the church door, then more and more hands smashed through the doors. Then the whole of the doors came crashing to the ground. All of a sudden, Ashley, Arron, Kyle and Sean fell down a trapdoor . . .

Down and down they fell then landed with a thud on a pit of bones. The walls started to close in. Arron got leg bones to stop the walls but the bones snapped. Then Arron saw a trapdoor but it disappeared.

Will they ever escape this horror in time?

Ashley Bailey (11)
Coleridge Primary School

A Day In The Life Of Ron Weasley

I woke up to the sound of the family ghost shaking his chains. He does it every morning about this time, Mum and Dad are really thinking about getting rid of him.

I turned on the light and saw Scabbers, my fat old rat Percy gave me, wriggling in his cage. It was the 13th day of June. It was the day we pick up Harry. Just then Mum shouted, 'Breakfast!' so I ran downstairs to the kitchen where I found Fred and George rubbing their eyes with tiredness and I sat next to them. Dad was reading 'The Daily Prophet' and Mum was washing up.

'Why did you shout us down Mum?' moaned Fred. 'Breakfast is not even ready.' Everyone was now sitting around the table.

We then all went upstairs and got dressed then came down looking more awake. Mum was standing at the fireplace holding a pot in her hands.
'Who's going first?' she said.
Travelling by floo powder meant we always got dirty. Fred nominated himself to go first, then George, then me.

In an instant, we were in a boarded-up fireplace. Dad took out his wand and said 'Flipendo!' The board flew off the fireplace and smashed into the radiator.

'Sorry,' Dad said to Harry's uncle.
Fred's pocket had just burst open and sweets were spread all over the floor.

Dudley pounced on the nearest one and stuffed it in his mouth and his tongue began to grow rapidly. Me and Harry jumped through the fireplace and back into my house.

Evan Ball (11)
Coleridge Primary School

THE LIBRARY

One night in Turkey, me, Bob and my friend Kyle felt sick. We went out for some air when suddenly lots of fog started to roll over the beach. We went to check it out. There was a big building there which had *Library* written just above the door. We moved a bit closer, it was an old library with broken windows. As we slowly crept forward, I heard a noise which came from behind me. I started to turn round slowly, Kyle's legs were moving from side to side. His teeth were bouncing up and down like a kangaroo who was hyperactive.

I told Kyle to be a bit quieter. We crept closer to the door when an old woman who had lots of wrinkles and long grey hair, appeared. Kyle said to her nicely, 'What's your name?'
She replied sweetly, 'Mrs Kilk. If you're going to go inside then you'll need this.' She gave me a horseshoe and she said, 'It'll always come back.' She gave Kyle some juggling balls and said, 'They'll always do what you tell them to.'

We went inside. Suddenly, *bang,* the door slammed shut, we tried to get out but couldn't so we looked and suddenly I heard another great big bang. I quickly turned round and there was a girl.
I shouted, 'What's your name?'
She replied, 'Eva!' She shouted again, 'Quickly, help me get out of here before the books get us.' We ran to help her. She wanted to knock the wall down, so I threw my horseshoe at the wall and it made a big hole. We quickly got out but then the books flew off the bookshelf and grabbed my foot. Kyle threw one of his juggling balls at the book and the book flew back and I got out quickly.

Suddenly Eva said, 'Duck!' I ducked and then Kyle's juggling ball flew past my head. We all went home and I told my mum but she didn't believe me but I know I was right.

Ryan Short (11)
Coleridge Primary School

A Day In The Life Of A Deckchair

It's cold, dark and gusty in here. We've been in this container, crammed in with hundreds of other deckchairs all winter and I just want to get out on to the beach and smell that fresh, sea air.

Click, click, clank, the door's opening, I can see a crack of lights gradually getting bigger. There's Dez, he's the man who looks after us and gives us to the holidaymakers for the day. At the moment, I'm at the back, so I will probably be picked last. My gran always used to say, 'Best till last!' But unfortunately she drifted out to sea.

As far as I can see Dez is unloading the front chairs. I'm at the top as well as at the back. So I can just make out a few things. Hey, what's this, a little girl screaming and shouting for a blue, no red and white chair. I can see Dez making his way over here. I can also see that I'm one of the few red and white chairs left.
'Right then Arnold!' said Des, picking up the chair in front of me. 'I'll have to move you, I need to get to Charlie (that's me).'
My hopes rose like the morning sun. Dez took me outside and showed me to the little girl.
'Oh yeah, oh yeah Daddy, I want that one!' she exclaimed.

Goody, goody, I've finally been picked. Every year when I get picked I'm ever so proud. Some of the other chairs think it's stupid but I just get that urge. Mmmm, I smell donuts, I smell candyfloss and fish and chips. I can see a lot more now - like fishing boats, rock pools, donkeys and not to mention, people.

I feel so much better now, I can smell that fresh sea air. But I'm not too sure about the girl. She's getting an ice cream . . . oh no, wait a minute, here she comes. *Splat!*
'Noooo! Daddy I dropped my ice cream on the stupid deckchair,' she yelled.

'Don't worry darling, sweetums! We'll get you another chair,' he said hurriedly. (I think that's because he didn't want the surrounding cliffs to fall down).

Now back to the point, my jolly, jolly mood perished out of my soul. They took me back to Dez and he was really nice about it. He just said that he'll wash me and that I'll be back on the beach tomorrow. So as you can imagine I am really pleased about that.

Hannah Dodson (11)
Dunswell Primary School

A Day In The Life Of A Deckchair

It was dark, cold and cramped. Squashed up against other deckchairs. We were piled up on top of each other, with nothing to do but sleep or look around the squashy chamber. We were trapped, then we heard huge footsteps coming towards us. We started to stare at the steel chamber doors. Who was it? What did they want? We didn't know what to expect.

The rusty metal bar was being slid across the door, the huge padlocks were unlocked. After all the noise of rusty bars and padlocks being moved, there was an eerie silence that not only did it make us wonder but it also made us scared. I noticed a thin, bright line between the doors, the doors opened wider and wider and wider until they were fully open!

Each one of us blinked in the light, we hadn't seen the daylight for six months. Just then two tall men started to get us out, one by one. I looked at the oldest of us all, Old Checkers. His cover was ripped and stained, his two back legs were broken. Would they repair him?

The two tall men lined us up ready for the people to hire us for the day, luckily I was at the back with my best friend.

Katie Martin (11)
Dunswell Primary School

A Day In The Life Of A Deckchair

Today it is the 26th of June 2003 and I have been in this rotten and dirty container for two years now and this morning I heard the people who own me (I'm the deckchair) say that at one o'clock they will be going to the beach they're taking me and look at the time. It's one o'clock right now, so any time now then, I'm off!

We stopped and I heard them get out of the car and *I'm out!* Ow, my eyes, by heck it's proper hot out here! Eh, now where are they taking me? Oh I remember now, they're taking me to the beach. Now here we are, oh god, this is boiling hot sand! The people who own me, opened me up onto the boiling hot sand just now!

Ooops! This is hot sand and the worst part is that I'm being sat on by a big fat man and he's really heavy! Good, he's just got off, but oh, now the children are here. Oh no, they've got ice creams and they've just spilled all of their ice cream all over me. Now I've had enough! But what can I do? Nothing but I can pray to make it rain so that the ice cream will wash off and then I can go home. I started to pray and then it started to rain and I said, 'Thank you.'

The ice cream came off and the people who owned me, grabbed me. They ran to the car and threw me into the back of the car. The car went really fast around the corners.

Finally, we were at home, they got out of the car and threw me into the garage and then they went into the house. Now I'm a bit wet but I'm glad I'm home but I don't want that to happen again, *ever!*

Ryan Hewitt (11)
Dunswell Primary School

A Day In The Life Of A Deckchair

It was a cold and frosty night in the enormous metal container for the poor, old, worn out deckchairs. They were looking forward to getting out into the warm, beautiful breezy, fresh air.

The next day they started to have really bad flashbacks. An extremely huge lady was squashed in one of them. He began to scream with fright. The chair next to him shouted, *'Get a hold of yourself!'*

Suddenly a light began to shine, like they remembered the sun. They all started cheering. 'Come on and choose a deckchair only £1 an hour, £8 a day.'

I saw the deckchair at the front, quivering, really excited because he knew that he would get chosen first and that he might be chosen by a really huge, overweight lady again.

From off the pier, a lady with four children began walking towards the shelter. I couldn't see the lady, I only knew that someone was there because I could hear the man say the prices again. When the lady came in view, I was really excited because the lady was thin. I was really excited and nervous.

But was I surprised when I came out of the shelter! I have been scraped and wrecked by being dragged on the floor. When I was eventually put up, the children started jumping and bouncing on me. I was really upset.

Snap! Crash! Bang! I lay broken. The chair had broken and the lady took me back and got her money back.

Finally the chair was thrown on the scrap pile with all the other broken deckchairs, which people like them have broken.

Stacey Celik (11)
Dunswell Primary School

A DAY IN THE LIFE OF A DECKCHAIR

It was the first day of summer and I was locked away. A bit of hope came my way because a sign was being put up, it said *Deckchairs £1 an hour.*

Finally a woman came, she wanted a deckchair, I felt on top of the world. I was stuck in the sand and a fat woman came and sat on me. Aching, I stretched, feeling as if I was going to split in two but at least I was in the sunlight - it felt great. Finally, she got up, I felt as if a great, big weight had been lifted off me. Then a seagull flew by and pooed on me, it was sickening.

When a child sat on me, he had an ice cream cone in his sandy hands, his ice cream fell on me and then I was dirty, then he got off me. I saw a ball in the air coming my way. It hit me and I was aching even more.

The sea was coming closer to me, everyone on the beach was leaving. The man was coming to put me back into that strange shed. He folded me up, I felt all cramped. He then unlocked the door and opened it, I saw the cobwebs and spiders and he finally put me in. I was thrown on top of a spider, it was crawling on me and tickling me. It was very dark and dull and dusty. I felt miserable and it was horrible in that storage shed.

Was I going to come out again? Nobody knows! My luck had gone.

Thomas Benson (10)
Dunswell Primary School

A Day In The Life Of A Deckchair

As I stood in the crowded and fusty-smelling container with plenty of other dusty deckchairs, the container was damp, dark and dull. There were also spiders' webs with millions of spiders on them all around the container.

As I tried to move in the cramped shed, something fell on me from the top of it and all of a sudden the door of the container swung open. The sun beamed in and stung my eyes and standing in the empty space was a tall but fat man. He reached in and grabbed me and many other deckchairs. I was nervous; I didn't have a clue what he was going to do to us. We came to a railing which was just above the yellow, hot sand. He dropped us and started shouting to everyone, 'Deckchairs for hire!'

During the time I was sitting on the pier, a skinny but tall man came over and picked up the deckchair next to me and started to walk off. A bit later on a fat, short lady, came up to the man who was hiring us out to people. She gave him some money and picked me up. I started to panic. I was so nervous. Where was she taking me? Where was I going?

After a long walk, the lady walked down some steep steps onto the beach with me. We eventually reached the bottom of the steps and she slammed me down on the sand. When she sat on me I started to sink into the sand. Then all of a sudden a teenager kicked a ball really hard and it hit me right in the centre of my red and white striped face, it started to throb. It was really hurting now.

Later on after a couple of hours of sunbathing with the lady, she eventually stood up and folded me together. I felt really stiff and tired. She put her shoes on and started the long journey up the steps again. We approached the top of the steps and the fat man was standing waiting with plenty of other deckchairs. The lady passed me back over to the man who snatched me off her.

He took me back to the container, opened the metal door and threw me into the back of the container. As he closed the door, I said to myself, 'Maybe next summer will be better!'

Laura Miller (11)
Dunswell Primary School

A Day In The Life Of A Deckchair

A container, a rotten old container, the sea was getting nearer.

I was stuck there for three whole months in a big, stacked pile and I was right at the bottom, really cramped and damp with all dust webs around me full of creepy-crawlies.

Then there was a sudden thud, I couldn't move. The sound was getting louder and louder until finally there I was, floating away in the swishing sea. It seemed relaxing, like a massage on my legs and arms. Although every now and again, we kept hitting rocks which made us uncomfortable. In the distance, I could see an island in the shape of a chair then as we got closer and cleaner too, we all got excited and started to argue with each other about who would be at the top. We spoke in squeak mode (our language).

After we hit a rock and everyone fell out - except me. I felt horrible and lonely because I couldn't help them and I felt that it was all my fault. I had an awful stomach ache.

When I got to the island I was refreshed but still couldn't let the thought of the others go out of my head. The ache was getting worse until a man and a woman came and got the deckchairs which had floated in onto the shore. They picked me up and stretched me out, she felt great on me! There was fresh air that I had never realised before. At last I would never be put into that smelly old container again, as she sat on me.

Jake Stead (10)
Dunswell Primary School

A DAY IN THE LIFE OF A DECKCHAIR

Hi, my name is Josh the deckchair - and this is my life.

One summer all of us deckchairs were put in a great big tin for the winter. We were in a massive pile and guess who was at the bottom . . . me!

Right at the top of the tin was a hole which we could look through, but I never had a chance to have a look because I was at the bottom. I didn't know what the world was like because when we were being put away, I was only a wee stool and I had eye problems and only after two weeks could my eyes see properly. I made a friend called Jim and we grew up together. He is only a week older than me.

One night, in the tin, the air felt warm, summer was coming. The next morning we were woken up by the rays of the sun shining through the door, opened by the man who put us in there in the first place. A fat man walked over and pointed at me and Jim.

'I'll take two.' He handed over some money and picked us up. We were taken over to some sand and then put down. He called to his wife, 'Honey, I've got 'em!'
'Lovely!' she said.

The lady sat on Jim and the man sat on me, but the man was so heavy he snapped my leg. The salesman came over and demanded the money and I got sent to the junk pile. I felt at home there and I married a gorgeous table and now we have twin stools, but I never saw my friend again.

Josh Clarkson (10)
Dunswell Primary School

A Day In The Life Of A Deckchair

Hi, I'm a deckchair called Mr Deckchair 300 and I live in a tin shed with lots of other deckchairs but the shed is cramped.

The tin shed I live in is damp and smells of rats and mice. Our wooden frames get damp and feel horrible. There are lots of cobwebs and it's very dusty in here as well. Every year I go in this tin shed and I hate it because rats and mice climb all over me.

Just then a car pulled up, I knew at once who it was. It was my owner, he owns all the deckchairs in the hire shop and he lets people borrow them. Suddenly the door opened, I could smell the fresh air, finally, I was saying in my head. I can also smell the sea and in the distance the sea roared as it hit the sand. I felt as if I'd started a new life. Suddenly I felt his hands grab me with a firm grip as he started lifting me up and put me next to a sign which said, *Deckchairs - £2 a day or 25p an hour.* Unfortunately it was a Sunday, so people might still be in bed, hopefully they're not though and they might pick me.

One hour later we were still waiting . . . five minutes later someone came. Oh no, they chose a different deckchair. In my head all that was going on was that I was hoping to get picked today and hopefully soon. Then I got bored because no one would speak to me because they all wanted to get picked as much as me.

After that, a big lady came with a young boy and she said that she wanted a deckchair and guess what? She chose me. Yes! She took me to the beach and laid on me, it was quite hard to keep upright. The only bad thing on the beach was that every time the lady sat on me, I had this terrible feeling that I was going to break (hopefully, I wouldn't). Just then I felt a horrible pain in my soft material, I had been broken! Then the baby needed changing and the big lady threw the nappy on me and guess what? It exploded open and all that yucky stuff came on me.

I had to be taken to the repair shop to be fixed and cleaned with Domestos. I was in there for a week because there were loads of other deckchairs needing to be fixed as well.

After being in the repair shop, I lived for another ten years and then I had to be thrown away.

Jonathan Clayden (10)
Dunswell Primary School

A Day In The Life Of A Deckchair

Hi, I'm deckchair 99 but you can call me Oddy. I'm cold and shivering all over my wood, cobwebs are sticking to my frame and I can smell rat poison.

Three months later, the door opened. Feeling relieved and excited I think we might not make it because some of my mates didn't make it, so that is why I'm scared, sitting here on top of the pier, I want to be picked first. I can smell the seaweed and the hot dogs and the fish and chips on me and all the other deckchairs can see lots of people. The seagulls are hovering over us and the rats are scurrying under all of us.

Another hour passes, finally I was happy that a man had picked me. I found some more people sitting down on some more deckchairs where the man put me down. He put me on some sand. There was a baby where the man put me down and he used me for a goal and he kept on doing it. It really hurt but I had to still be the goal because deckchairs can't talk. The next thing he did was he jumped on me and I broke. I felt really bad where the boy had hurt me. The man said I would have to be repaired because they had paid some money for me and they had paid for all day. So he took me back and said to the man, 'I want my deckchair fixed now!'
So the man said, 'Give me an hour and I will have it fixed for you.'
The man agreed and he sat on the sand feeling sad and grumpy whilst I got fixed.

The man took me to a big repair place, I think it is called a factory and they gave me a new cover - so I was repaired. He didn't take me back to the man who'd broken me, he put me back into the container for another six months. *What a day!*

Mark Hostick (10)
Dunswell Primary School

A Day In The Life Of A Deckchair

One cold night in a shed, I was folded up. It was crowded and dark, cold, rotten, stinky and creepy with rats and mice. I didn't like it very much because I was in there for six months. The next day it was normal and suddenly the door opened, it was summer.

I was the first to come out, it was too sunny and it was so hot that my blue and white stripes faded.

I was chosen by a big man but I was surprised because his little son sat down on me. The little boy ran off and played in the wet sand near the water. He ran back to me and he had an ice cream and I felt miserable. He dropped the ice cream, I was a right mess. I'd got a new cover when I was ripped after I came out.

The man said, 'I want to go now.' So the man gave the chairs back and the man put me in first. It was late now and I was still awake because I was very, very squashed. It was the last day of summer and it was cold.

The new cover which I got was white and red. It was night and we stayed in the shed for another six months. After the six months, we were out in the sunshine again. But after two days my cover got ripped again and the man threw me in the rubbish bin.

Another man found me and he got another cover, it was blue and white. He took me home and he sat on me. He sat on me for an hour when suddenly *crash!* I fell to bits and he put me in the bin again.

Becky Lovelock (9)
Dunswell Primary School

A Day In The Life Of A Deckchair

Hi, I'm Dudly Deckchair, my life is so boring! I'm stuck in a tin can. Every day I wait for somebody to pick me. The tin can is wet, damp and really creepy, not forgetting - very dark! Every morning I wake up and look at the misty cobwebs.

Finally, the door opened. I felt the sea breeze on the frame of my back. I could smell the salt and vinegar in my mouth.

All of a sudden I got chosen and guess what it was? It was a fat person. It was awful, I couldn't breathe, it was horrible. The woman got up and she put her baby on me and it was sick on me. I thought, *yuck!* It was disgusting. A man in a yellow suit came and hosed me down, then he dried me off with a towel, I was freezing, then he blow-dried me. By the end of that, I was really, really tired. It was a long and hard day. Then the man came back but for some reason he didn't take me to the tin can, I don't know why!

Then another person came with triplets. One of them had an accident on me. It was disgusting. I had an incredible smell on me. The lady changed her but I didn't feel any better because I still really smelt. So again the man hosed me down again. My deckchair frame was shivering. I got dried off and finally I went back into the tin shed.

Bobby Taylor (10)
Dunswell Primary School

A DAY IN THE LIFE OF A DECKCHAIR

Hi, I'm Deckchair 2000. I'm the youngest deckchair in town but the best.

It was the last day of winter, we were all excited. Meanwhile, the next day a fat man opened the doors and scared us totally.

When he got us out of the container and put us outside of the pier, I could smell the fresh air and the salty sea and fish and chips.

Suddenly loads of people came to rent a deckchair for the day. I was stuck with a fat man, trust me! After that a bird messed on me and a child was sick on me. He spilled ketchup on me and snapped me. I was really hurt, so bad I got thrown away.

Dean Steer (10)
Dunswell Primary School

A DAY IN THE LIFE OF A DECKCHAIR

It was another cold winter's day in the tin box. I was on the top of all the deckchairs. I am one of the youngest deckchairs in the box and I have been in this box for six months.

It is cold, smelly, dusty and a bit creepy, but next week I come out of the box, it will be the happiest day of my life. My best friend is now at the bottom of the box. I can't wait to see him. His name is Jim and my name is Joe. It's warm and I come out.

Today I can't wait to feel the smooth, shiny sand and the waves crashing and the birds singing. I sure do hope I don't get a rotten person, there is only two more hours to go until I get the sun on my blue and white stripes.

Well here I am, the sun is shining and I have a clean person on me and guess who is next to me? Yes Jim! But then the man had a hot dog with lots of ketchup on and he dropped some on me. It went all over but the man got a new cover with red and black stripes.

Sam Oliver (10)
Dunswell Primary School

A GHOST STORY

One year ago, a little girl saw a strange castle on the way home. She thought it was weird as she had never seen it before. She thought about going inside and the next day she went inside.

So now she was in, she looked round and saw something moving. So what did she do? She ran of course, she ran like the wind. She did not tell her parents, they would have a fit.

The next day she went with her friends again and they saw three mangled bodies. She recognised one, it was her teacher. Just then the door slammed and it would not open an inch. They screamed as a lady came and she asked them, 'Would you like some sweets?'
'Yes!' they replied.
They ate the sweets and fell asleep.

One woke up and screamed. None of them awoke and so she was stabbed to death and the lady dispersed into thin air . . .

Oh did I forget to say that the little girl was me?
Ha! Ha! Ha!

Katherine McQue (9)
Mill Hill CP School

THE RIVER MYSTERY

Stickelback River was a dark, creepy place, no one barely ever went there. Chris and Joe were supposed to be going down for a swim there but little did they know what they were in for.

'Here it is!' Joe exclaimed.
They came to a big cluster of trees next to the river.
'What was that?'
'What?'
'That rustle in the trees.'
'Joe, don't you feel like someone's watching us?'
'Yeah, it's creepy.' Joe replied.
'Come on let's just enjoy ourselves and swim.'

They jumped into the murky water of Stickelback River.

'It's freezing!' Chris shivered.
'Don't be a wuss,' said Joe and he splashed Chris all over his head. As they were laughing and playing, something lurked a few metres away.
Splosh!
'Joe, you must have heard . . . '
'Argh!' Chris was pulled down below the water surface.
'Chris!' Joe grabbed his arm and pulled with all his might.
'Keep . . . pulling,' Chris spluttered.
'There!' After many minutes Chris laid on the bank, panting like a dog.

Suddenly the monster thing, creature or whatever it was, climbed out of the water.
'Run!' they shouted together. Chris and Joe sprinted up the hill, down the lane and into the safety of their house.

'I'm never going there again,' coughed Chris and flopped onto the sofa.

Joseph Price (11)
Sinnington Primary School

MASS MURDER

The steward looked down the empty lane after the football match. A large bruise was growing on his face and he was tired and cross.

His flat was in a large ruined block. After much grumbling, he was woken up to screaming and shouting when a blood-splattered arm came down the window. He froze in his tracks. When he caught his breath again, he ran faster than lightning. Down, down, down the metal steps. The sight was terrifying.

Ambulances, fire, police - they all looked as baffled as he did. Everybody lay dead in the street and four men in black suits jumped into a van and drove off. The police chased them but they soon got away. They were cross as they knew that the killers had already killed in two cities in Texas and now they had escaped to Florida and had killed again.

He couldn't sleep. 'They know that I saw their faces and they can't risk my knowing them,' he said to himself.

Bang! Bang!
'Argh!' the steward cried as rivers of blood poured from his head.
Another, but quieter *bang!*
The steward was dead!

'Man killed!' hit the headlines fast.

Eloise Davison (11)
Sinnington Primary School

A Day In The Life Of A Cat

I was kicked outside today (as usual). I had a saucer of milk and a bowl of cat food for breakfast. Sorry, I'm a bit tired. I've just been chased by a dog. That dog has just got no sense of humour. I just said he was looking a bit flabbier than usual. Actually I said, 'What did you have for breakfast, you're looking awfully fat.' He didn't catch me. That piece of blubber couldn't hurt a fly.

Oh by the way, my name is Ralph. Okay, I'll tell you about my life.

I eat, sleep and stare up into space all day, but at night, my friends and I have a party. Most nights, after the party, we sit on my garden wall and yowl and wake people up. It's actually quite good fun. Do you know what my favourite thing to do is? Run into the road when a car is coming. Oh sorry, I have to go now, it's lunchtime.

Jordan Brown (10)
Sinnington Primary School

HAUNTED HOUSE

Hi, I am Rosalie and this is my story and my friend Ruby as well.

Ruby came over to my house and we were bored so we went to explore this abandoned house. We crept up some stairs. There were ghouls that looked like they were guarding the house and were going to jump out and grab us. We edged in.

Suddenly some kind of mummy fell out of a mouldy cupboard. Its head fell off and rolled down the creaking floorboards. Its finger seemed to be pointing at the rolling head. I nudged Ruby and we followed it. Then I saw a shadow and heard footsteps. Ruby and I were looking at each other terrified.
'Let's get out of here,' I said.

Then we turned round to run but the door jammed shut. I ran to it and started to kick it and rattle the handle. By this time we were screaming and shouting for help because the footsteps were getting closer.

Suddenly the door swung open. We felt slimy cold hands wrapping around our necks. I automatically grabbed the arms and pulled it off. They were lying in my hands. We realised what it was. Then we ran for our lives and we never went there again.

Rosalie Sampson (10)
Sinnington Primary School

THE BIG MURDER

Once there was an old lady who lived on her own in a flat.
Knock, knock, knock, knock!
'Alright I'm coming.' She opened the door.
Bang! The old lady dropped slowly to the floor with blood dripping from her forehead.

Three days later the police heard about the murder. They got straight on to the case. The Superintendent immediately went to the old lady's flat. Forensics were there. When the Super got there she put on her white suit, there were rivers of blood everywhere. It was horrible!

She, the Super, went into the kitchen and there was the gun. The Super could really see the fingerprints. She asked a couple of the forensic people to come over and take it away.

1st May 2003. Police station:

'Everyone, could you just please crowd round me. Now as you all know, we've got a murder investigation on our hands. One particular suspect is Mr Dean Matthews. He's 23 years of age. Now he has done one or two different things to people before. He has murdered twice and beheaded once.'

One of the policemen looked out of the window and there he was! They ran down the metal steps and caught him. The policeman said, when they caught him, 'Dean Matthews, I am arresting you on the suspicion of murder. You do not have to say anything but anything you do say will be taken into court.' He then took Dean Matthews upstairs and through the wooden doors.

'Ladies and gentlemen I think we've got him!'

James Jeavons (9)
Sinnington Primary School

A Day In The Life Of A Fox

'My name is Foxy. Everyone calls me Fox, so you can too. I suppose I should tell you a bit about myself. I love hiding from people, it's fun. I'm a black fox dog and I have seven cubs called Molly, Dan, Can, Su, Nan, Pap and the runt (Runt).

I know you're thinking what kind of foxes call cubs names like these. In the fox world there's a law that you have to call them certain names. My wife is called Harriet.

Did I tell you that my best friend is a pigeon? He gets really annoying, so I went and killed him and stuffed him with apple sauce. I really want to eat him but I can't, it would be cruel.

I've got a collection of woodlice. I'm going to give it to Runt. He loves beetles.

I must have forgotten to tell you where I live. Well I live in a den called Granny Ville where all the old people live. We don't mind they're really kind to the little ones.

I've heard something, it's a poacher. I'd better go or it's bye-bye to me. See you soon I hope. If you see me around, give me a wave.

Erin Smith (10)
Sinnington Primary School

HOLIDAY HORROR

I was at a Holiday Hotel when strange things started to happen.

It all started when I asked the waitress for a chocolate muffin. The waitress came back with a speck of *blood* on a small dish! After that I went back to my room for a wash. I got the flannel and put it in the water and as I was washing my face I looked in the mirror above the sink. My face started to feel a bit clammy. A I lifted my face up to look, there was mud and worms all over it!

The next day I went to the reception to complain about the incidents. The receptionist said, 'Oh what a shame, we will put you in another room.' As she said it she sounded almost robotic! So she gave me the key and I entered the tacky room.

I looked inside the room and there were all the staff but they looked different somehow. One of the staff turned around, looking in my direction. If he'd seen me, who knows what would have happened, but he looked like a *vampire!*

Ruby Williams (9)
Sinnington Primary School

A DAY IN THE LIFE OF AUGUSTUS KING OF THE DARK

Augustus the zombie, King Of The Dark stands at the top of the mountain. The huge eye on his right shoulder flashes. His black cloak hangs down his back. He is growling like thunder.

He uses his evil, dark power to bring the zombies back from the dead. They are all around the world. He flies with his magic cloak to visit them all.

Augustus grabs a dead zombie with his claw-like hands and bites them with his sharp teeth. The zombies slowly come back to life.

Augustus and the zombies start to attack the people and to drink their blood. The people then turn into zombies. Eventually, only two people are left alive. They hide in a dark, damp cave full of guns. Augustus comes into the cave, clashing teeth and roaring, 'You have been into my cave of the zombies, you will go and be one of us!'
The man shoots Augustus with a bazooka. *Bang!*

Augustus is dead. All the zombies turn back into human beings and the world is saved.

Thomas Booth (10)
Sinnington Primary School

Man At The Window

I was walking along and I saw an old man watching me. He disappeared and I ran home. All night I sat and thought and in the morning I went into the room where he was last night.

I saw the most dreadful sight in my whole life. He lay dead and his eyes were missing, his ears had been cut off and he had no legs.

I walked in and there was blood all over the walls, and there was a massive carving knife on the floor. I picked it up and a hand came out of the wardrobe and grabbed me on the shoulder.

'Get off!' I shouted and turned round. He had a gun to my head and out came a police officer.
'What are you doing here?' he whispered.
'What are you doing?' I replied.
'I'm a policeman, I'm always at the crime.'
'Where's your badge then?' I asked.
'I forgot it,' he said.
'Then you're not a police officer today if you've forgotten it. You're a murderer aren't you?'
'Yes!' came a creepy voice as he turned into a cloaked murderer. I tried to run but he simply stuck out his hand and I tripped up. He tied my legs up.

The next week . . .

'I'll get you for this,' he said as he was taken away by the real police.
'I'll get you one day!'
'No you won't, you're going to prison forever.' I replied.

Edward Bell (10)
Sinnington Primary School

SAVING CIVILIAN RYAN

Norway 1940

The man-carriers were on their way. The civilians had all been killed, all except Ryan. The men who were not used to war puked all over the carriers. They landed and the ramp went down. Bullets ricochet into the carrier. People tried to get out but they got shot.

The captain said, 'Jump over the side.'
When the Germans realised that they'd jumped over the side they shot into the water. Two men were shot and another one drowned. The water turned red.

The captain gathered up survivors and ran to a pile of sand. A mortar bomb blew up and someone's legs came off! The captain ran to the giant pillbox, he only had a quarter of his men left. There was a sandbagged bunker with two machine guns and two mortars, but they had two bazookas. They fired and blew them up but the Germans had twenty guns and twenty *tanks!* The captain only had twenty men left so they had to surrender. The mission failed.

Stewart Cambridge (10)
Sinnington Primary School

A Day In The Life Of A Fly

Hello, Fly here! Do you want to listen to a day of my life? You do! That's fantastic and here it goes.

One day I was having a wonderful dream when I got woken up by a big, big shadow. I looked up and saw a *massive fly swatter!*

Hello! Phew! That was close. Luckily I escaped and I looked back and stuck my tongue out at the swatter and then I flew into something sticky. I couldn't escape. I looked the other way and there was a horrible *spider!*

Suddenly a human came in and said, 'I thought I told you to tidy up this mess.'
Phew! There's Miss Honeysuckle, she dusted me free. I'm saved *hooray! Hooray! Hooray!* I flew outside and landed on the wall. Then a *huge* face came up to me. It's a *cat!* I flew so far, I flew to France, so that was a day in my life.

Amy Fisher (9)
Sproatley Endowed School

A DAY IN THE LIFE OF A FLOWER PETAL

Hello, I'm a flower petal called Blossom and I live outside with my brothers and sisters, but I'm stuck on a flower. Uh oh, a girl's coming to pick my friends and me up, *Argh!*

She's taken us home, home with her. Now what's she doing? She's putting us in water. Argh! We're drowning, help!

Hey what's that? Hey, I'm flying! Wee, uh oh, argh! Ow! Ooh! My head, I really hurt myself then. I banged into a door ooh! Ow! Ee! Oh!

Oh no, that girl's come back. Now she's picking me up. Argh! Ow! Ooh! Ee! I think I'm safe. Uh oh! A kid on a skateboard. Argh! Move, c'mon! Woo! Hoo! I'm alive. I'm back on the floor, on the grass and I'm asleep. Hhhhooo! Ssshhhooo!

Aimie Louise Rendle (8)
Sproatley Endowed School

A Day In The Life Of A Woodlouse

Hello, I am a woodlouse called Willow. I live on a table with plenty of things to do. Wow! What's that? The table's moving - argh! What's that? Ouch! I am getting swept up.

Eeeww, a mouldy banana. I don't want to be in here for long. Who switched off the lights? Wow! Ouch, don't you realise I am in here? Oo! Ah! Oo! Ah! It's bouncy in this car.

I think I am getting thrown in the air. Ouch! I must be on the ground again. What's that coming towards me? Oh no! It's a car! I am stuck. I must be stuck to something, I am getting dizzy. Wow! Hey! I am on some wood again. I am happy.

Emma Upfield (8)
Sproatley Endowed School

A Day In The Life Of A Piece Of Flapjack

I am a piece of flapjack. I'm in Asda waiting to be bought. It's nice and comfy in my jar. Argh! all of my mixture's swooshing about. Someone's picked me up. Ow! I banged my head. Ow, it happened again. Uh, I'm getting very dizzy.

Now I'm being put into a car. It's even more swooshy and bangy. Ouch, my head, you should have heard that clang, it was the loudest one I've ever heard in my life. Uh, now I'm going over lots of bumps. *Jig, jig.* There's lots of bags in here with other things in them like carrots (it said on the packet) and cheese (it said that on the packet as well). Ow, we've stopped. Aah! Someone's taking me out. Oh no, ouch! Someone dropped me. *Phew!* They've picked me up again. I've been taken inside.

Plop! Plop! I'm now in a bowl. Aah, round and round I go. Phew, I've stopped. Oh no, now they're putting me into a thing with a door. Ow, it's hot. It's getting even hotter, it's *boiling!* Ow, ow, my bottom. I'm on a tray inside something boiling hot. *Ouch! Ouch!*

Phew, they've taken me out. Thank goodness for that. There's a blade. *Ouch!* Ooohhh, that hurt so much. I'm in something really cold. I'm shaking, it's so cold in here. On the front of the door it said it was a fridge. Now they're taking me out. *Splat!* I'm in a box, the light's going out. *Click.*

Emily Gilroy (9)
Sproatley Endowed School

A DAY IN THE LIFE OF A BONE

Hello, I am a little bone and I live on a shelf in a pet shop. I'll tell you what happened to me. One day, I was sitting on the shelf with my friends and then suddenly, a lady grabbed me and put me in a bag. I think I got taken into a house. Suddenly, I heard a rattling noise. It was paper coming round me. I think I got strangled by a ribbon. It was very tight and hot while I was wrapped in there. Ow! I just got thrown on the floor, a very hard floor.

While I was there I could see light, but feel rain. It wasn't rain, it was a dog slobbering all over me. He started to bite me. He started to chew me. *Ouch, ooh, aah!* He started to carry me somewhere and then he started to roll me in dirty mud and grass. It was horrible.

A hand grabbed me and put me into a bin. Yuck. Mouldy banana skins and a sticky apple, and lots of sharp, broken glass.

Somebody started to lift up the bag I was in. They put me into a machine which put a stamp on me. Then I got put on a stinky pile of rubbish. There were all these mouldy things around me.

Just then, a dog came up and licked me and took me to a pet shop. That's where I am today. I am very happy here.

Brogan Taylor (9)
Sproatley Endowed School

A DAY IN THE LIFE OF A TENNIS BALL

I am a tennis ball and I live on a shelf. It is hard being a tennis ball. Oh no! Something has fallen. I'm rolling off the shelf. Help! I'm bouncing on the floor. Wait! What is that? I'm being taken somewhere. Help, someone. Help!

Hey! Where am I? *Oh no*! I'm getting thrown into space. Wait, what's this? A tree! *Crash!* Ow, that hurt. Wait! What's that? It's a dog. Look at those fangs. hey, it's eating me. It's taking me somewhere. Help! *Cough, cough.* Where am I? It's dark. Hey, someone's picking me up. Not again. Help!

Aaah, back on my shelf. Yawn! I'm going to sleep. *Bang!* Hey! What's that disturbing my sleep? Stupid noise. Hey! I'm rolling away! Not again. Help! I'm not rolling. Hey! You're a cricket ball, nice to meet you. We can be friends forever.

Adam Mearns (9)
Sproatley Endowed School

A Day In The Life Of A Leaf

Hello, Laura the leaf speaking here and I'm nice and cosy hanging on my tree with all my friends. But wait, I heard something. There it goes again. Phew, it's gone. Argh! Maybe not. *Help!* I'm blowing away.

Thump! Ow. That hurt. Oh no, I've landed on the front of a car window and I'm trapped by the windscreen wipers. This is the worst day I've ever had.

Blob! Blob! Oh great, it's starting to rain. What a surprise. Wait a minute, if I'm trapped by the windscreen wipers and it's raining, that means . . . argh! I'm getting really dizzy. Oh, I think I'm going to be sick. *Help!* I want my mummy. *Help!* Oh, it's stopped. Yeah, it's gone.

Ouch! Ouch! Stop pricking me. Hooray, the bird saved me! Whee! I'm flying with the bird.

Bump! Hey, be careful. I'm very delicate. Oh, they're so cute and they've only just hatched. I think I want to live here forever.

Laura Wood (9)
Sproatley Endowed School

A Day In The Life Of A Golf Ball

I am a golf ball and I live in my owner's comfy, warm and fluffy golf bag. I have just woken up and I am still a little bit tired. Wait a minute, I hear something. I think it's my owner. It's getting louder. Aah! It feels like I'm in a car. Wait a minute, I am in a car. Ow, slow down, I feel dizzy.

That's better, it's not bumpy anymore. Hey, it's cold now, I'm on the floor. Ow, that hurt. *Plop.* I've fallen into the pond. Help! Something's poking me. Ah, that's better. I'm out of the pond, dry land again. Hooray. That's better, I'm back in my comfy golf bag.

Here we go again, back in the bumpy car. Hey, I think we have stopped. Yes, we have stopped at long last. I'm home. I hope I can have some sleep now. Aaah, that's very relaxing. I'm glad I'm home.

Sarah Barry (8)
Sproatley Endowed School

A DAY IN THE LIFE OF A PEN

I'm Penny the pen, and I'm sitting in my basket, all warm and comfortable with my friends.

If you want, I'll tell you a story that once happened to me. Well here I go. I was sitting in my basket, nice and warm, and suddenly someone took me from my warm basket and I was really scared. Well, I was all right after a while, but I was used so much that I got thrown in the bin. I had run out of ink. But then I began to go all weak and someone said, 'Mrs Green, the bin needs emptying.'
'OK,' she said, and walked to the bin. When she came over, she saw me and took me home. Mrs Green started scribbling again, but I didn't work, so she threw me in the bin.

I wasn't very happy because there were snotty tissues and scratchy edges and apple cores and horrid stuff like that. I got away, but I landed on a leaf and went down the drain. *'Whee,'* I said, but I was back at school in my basket, nice and warm. I don't know how. Do you?

Ciara Dudley (9)
Sproatley Endowed School

A DAY IN THE LIFE OF MAISY MARBLE

Yo, Maisy Marble here. Do you want to listen to a very, and I mean *very*, exhausting day? You do! Really! Honestly! Wow! Nobody ever wants to listen to boring old me. I'll do my best, here it goes.

One morning I was asleep in my matchbox with all of my colourful friends. I was very uncomfortable and I was squashed, but I did manage to sleep. I was nice and snug, when all of a sudden, *bang! Crash! Shake!* Oh no! A stream of light filled the matchbox and I woke with a shock!

Aarrghhh! What's that? Oh, it's freezing! Goodness, it was one of those giant hand things. *Help! Help!* It's picking me up. Oww! Ouch! hey! Stop that. Now they're playing with me. Hey, stop! Stop! Heeeelp!

Oh phew, I have a headache. Oh, I'm rather hot now. Wait a minute, oh, it's gone all dark now. Why, I think I'm in a pocket. Yes, I am. *Waaaa*, I don't like it. Ooooo, mmmm, I've fallen in a pile of biscuits, I'm in a big biscuit tin.

Where am I now? I don't like Saturdays anymore. Oh, finally, I'm in my matchbox again. Thank goodness. Nighty night!

Helena Saul (9)
Sproatley Endowed School

ESCAPING

'What, where am I? What am I?'

'You're here,' said a sly voice. 'You're with Madam Lulu!'

I jump up in horror; Madam Lulu is a recluse. She's an evil witch, what can I do? I jump again, but I go really high this time. I build up the courage to look down. *'Help!'* I scream. 'Oh my goodness, I'm a rabbit. Help!' I jump, I scram, fall, I hide, but Madam Lulu is one step behind me all the way. The door, I can see the door. I'm so close, I'm there, I'm free.

'I'll get you if it's the last thing I do,' cries Madam Lulu.

I jump away in terror until finally I hear a familiar noise of someone banging pots and pans. Home, I'm home. I hop to the front door and knock (with my teeth).

'Hello,' says a sly voice, 'nice of you to join me.'

Oh no, I'm trapped. Not again. Not again. It's Madam Lulu. *Oh no!* Suddenly, loud noises fill the sky. *Bang, bang, bang.*

'What's happening?' cries Madam Lulu.

'What's happening?' I cry.

I'm getting bigger. Madam Lulu's getting smaller. She's a hamster and I'm me again! I grab her and shove her in a nearby cage.

'Let me out!' screams Lulu.

I pretend not to hear her and stroll inside. 'Night,' I shout, 'goodnight.'

Emily Monaghan (11)
Wharncliffe Side Primary School

THE LIFE OF AN OLD FRIENDLY PONY

Hi, I'm Danny, a fifteen-year-old pony belonging to Jane Smith. I've got lovely brown fur and shiny brown eyes. I live at a farm and I'm well looked after. My owners feed me delicious food which I eat every night before I sleep with my three friends, Tosker, Cassy and Keeper. Cassy's my favourite friend as I've known her the longest.

When it's winter, I get to go in the stable and cuddle up in the warm hay until morning. We all play together, and although Tosker hates Keeper, it is still very peaceful. We have a big field to play in. It's brilliant, the sun always shines down on us and we have lots of privacy at the bottom of the field, to sleep or gaze. Unfortunately, I can't ride anymore as I am too old and am not strong enough to go a long way, maybe just up or down the road. I get lonely and a bit jealous sometimes when the other horses go riding and leave me on my own. When they're gone, I often dream of the old days when I used to ride with my friends. I still run though, which is brilliant, especially when I've got my friends with me. Talking about friends, they're back, bye. *Neigh!*

Rachel Revitt (10)
Wharncliffe Side Primary School

A NIGHT IN THE LIFE OF TWITCHY

Yo, you. I'm Twitch. It's night-time and I'm on a mission to break free of this cage. It just isn't fair. I try all the time to get out, but it isn't working. When my owner gets me out, it's time to run. He doesn't stand a chance of catching me.

The annoying thing is, he never gets me out when I'm awake, but only when I'm asleep and tired. Food is not a luxury to me because I get it all the time. I communicate with other hamsters to plan our escape and finally be free.

The other hamsters have smaller cages than me, so I have to climb further up to get out of my cage. It's hard for me to escape, because I'm two human years old. I can remember when I escaped from my old cage. My owners had to put me in a red toy box filled with sawdust for a week. Now I've got my big blue cage, which is harder to break through.

I clean myself about twenty times a night to get rid of parasites and fleas. I love my family, but I hate my owner's brother, because he slavers on me all the time.

Phil Webster (11)
Wharncliffe Side Primary School

A ROMANCE STORY

'When I saw her face, I felt like a poet.'

'Keep going, Grandfather, it sounds so romantic.'

'Oh, all right then. So, as a romantic tune played, I walked up to her and asked, "Marie, will you marry me?"

It was stupid at the time, but then she said, "*Yes!* But come, hurry, run away with me. Come on, we shall take my father's boat!"

We were childhood dream-hearts, and now this was my chance to love her dearly.

"Hurry!"

"Why are we hurrying?"

"Because tonight, I was supposed to have met my groom, Lord Hawk. He is a horrible man. Now, come, hurry!"

When we got the boat I turned around and Lord Hawk was chasing us with guards behind him. He looked mad. Lord Hawk was only marring her for her money.

"Quick, get in the boat. Hurry!"

As we got in the boat, we didn't know that a boat was next to ours.

"Row Jonathan!"

I rowed and rowed, but the guards were to strong. Then *bang!* Lord Hawk banged his boat into ours and . . .

"Help!" Marie fell in the water.

"Marie!" . . . I couldn't move, breathe, be angry. I felt my heart beating loud and clear. I even thought that the guards could hear my heartbeat. I dived in and tried to find her, but when I saw the last bubbles, I gave up and swam to the shore.

Lord Hawk spat on the floating body, then drifted away.

'A few years later, I met your grandmother and we married. You could say we lived happily ever after.'

Annabel Groves-Taylor (10)
Wharncliffe Side Primary School

GHOST STORY

Nicola and her three friends Lauren, Michelle and Sarah, were having a walk in the woods, when they came to a clearing. They could see an old house. The old red bricks were worn, most of the roof slates were missing and the windows were smashed. It looked like no one had been there in years.

Then they saw Tanya running out of the house as fast as she could; she was too scared to talk. They went to see what was wrong. Had she seen something beyond imagination?
'What did you see?' Sarah asked.
'Something's in that house,' Tanya replied, 'I don't know what it is, but I never want to see it again.'
'What's wrong?' Nicola asked.
'I saw old pictures, they were of dead people. They were being hanged, burnt and executed. They all started moving. The hanged one was swinging. The fire on the burnt one was moving and the head rolled off the executed one. It was really horrible.'

They were thinking about whether to go and investigate the house or keep away. It was a tough decision to make, but they had to decide. They looked at the possibilities. Should they go in and maybe die, or stay out and have the chance of living? They decided to stay away, so they turned around to go home. Then Nicola turned around and so did the rest of them, and saw a pale face in the window and they ran off screaming.

Stephanie Duignan (11)
Wharncliffe Side Primary School

THE RETURN OF ZOMBIE JACK

Once upon a time on the outskirts of Skimvil, was the grave of Jack. Harriet, his next-door neighbour, had used a sledgehammer and knocked off Jack's head following an argument over the height of his new garden fence.

And now Jack had risen from the grave in search of revenge on Harriet. Far away at the TV station, the TV presenter, Mr Bowman, said, 'We interrupt this programme to bring you the Zombie Jack Show.' By the time Mr Bowman had explained, Jack had just reached Harriet's house. Then Jack knocked a hole in the door. He put his head through and shouted, 'Here's Jackie.' Then he just walked straight through the door without a care. When Jack found Harriet, he raised his bat ready to hit her. But just then, Laura jumped through the window with a laser gun. 'Back off, slimeball!' And Laura blew a hole in Jack.

Then from that day forward, they lived happily ever after.

Michael Draycott (11)
Wharncliffe Side Primary School

A Day In The Life Of A Ghost

I'm going to show you what an ordinary day is like as a ghost.

Knock, knock. That's how the day usually starts, with some annoying child that's been dared to come and knock on my door. Well, like always, I go and answer the door, *'Boo!'* They run away as fast as their legs will carry them; like idiots.

The good thing about being a ghost is that you don't have to eat, sleep or waste time on the toilet all day, so when it's gone midnight I can spook the new next-door neighbours.

Ding-dong, ding-dong, the clock strikes twelve. Yes, they'll be sorry.

I walk slowly towards the neat brick house and bash on the green front door and fly away quickly to the back door and bash on that manically, but this time I don't run away. I stand there waiting, waiting with a butcher's knife in my hand.

Suddenly, someone opens the door quickly. I try to chop the woman's head off, but she is too quick and slams the door in my face, screaming. 'I'll be back, I'll get you back for turning me into a ghost,' I say, looking through the cracked window.

Holly Swinden (11)
Wharncliffe Side Primary School

HORROR BIRTHDAY

It as my 11th birthday, a day I would never forget (for all the wrong reasons). My mum had made a delicious cake, using an old recipe book. It had little purple lilies and sugar letters.

I took a bite from the mouth-watering cake. Everything grew bigger, or I shrank smaller. Everything looked weird: Mum, the table and the carpet looked like the ocean, far and wide.

I climbed up the chair leg onto the table and started screaming at my mum. She quickly ran to one of the cupboards and grabbed the old recipe book. She flicked through the book to find the page.

Meanwhile, I read the title. It was covered in dust. I wiped away the dust and it said, 'Cursed Cakes'! I screamed and nearly fainted. My mum found the page she was looking for. She showed the page to me. I read the small print.
'Mum, if any person eats the cake, they will become ten times smaller. They only have 24 hours to make the drink to reverse the curse. Quick, turn to page 198!'

Mum and I worked all night but we could only find some tinned strawberries, instead of fresh, but they were the only ones we could find and I didn't have time to run to the shops.

I drank it all. It tasted of lemons and toffees, tastes I like on their own, but together they're horrible. Everything grew back to normal luckily, the minute before doom.

Kathryn Dewsnap (11)
Wharncliffe Side Primary School

WHITBY SHIVERS

It was a foggy day in Whitby, when Rob and Kate were walking Fluff right at the edge of the cliff. The street was silent and still, with people snug in their beds, dreaming of happy thoughts. Suddenly, the cliff edge started to crumble and Kate was hanging of with one hand, terrified and frightened. 'Help!' she trembled. 'Help, lift me up Rob, save me!'
Rob tried to pull her up, but slid down, and he was now hanging off with one hand, with the other one holding Kate's hand.
'Go and find someone, Fluff!' he shouted.
Fluff went running off, but by the time he came back, Kate was lying dead on the rocks, about to be washed up. He had come back with the children's family, who were tired but scared.

Suddenly, a big wave came and Rob fell down.
'I'm going to die with my children!' cried their mum, who jumped off the cliff.
'Don't go!' shouted their dad. But of course, she was already dead.

One month later, Father and Fluff, who were still alive, were walking on the path and saw two children and an adult woman, all playing happily at the cliff edge. 'Kate, Rob, Mother!' he cried.
They looked at him, then carried on playing. They turned to look at him again and came towards him. They hugged each other, but with a gigantic bite at the neck, Father was now dead. The ghosts had eaten Father that day. Fluff ran back home, alone.

Amy Leighton (11)
Willerby Carr Lane Junior School

CREEPY-CRAWLIES

'Creepy-crawlies do not harm you,' said Bob.

Bill moved where there were no creepy-crawlies, but he sat on a lot of millipedes and centipedes. 'Bob, I sat on something, but I don't know what it is,' said Bill.

Bob whispered, 'You're sat on millipedes and centipedes.

'Argh!' screamed Bob. 'Get them off me, argh! Quick, get the vacuum cleaner.'

'No silly, they won't come off.'

Bob went upstairs and went into a bedroom and screamed, 'Help, there's spiders crawling all over me.' So he ran downstairs and they both ran outside and bumped into something. When they ran outside, it was raining quite fast, with hailstones, but they got home safely and never went to the creepy house again.

Sean Rose (11)
Willerby Carr Lane Junior School

AGGRESSION POSSESSION

Long ago, there was an evil man who ruled the town of Costland. The man was called Frank Easter, but bunnies weren't his style. And me, I was hiding from the police. I mean, all I did was burn down the hospital and the supermarket, what's the harm in that?

Anyway, I was running through Lowrule Field when I saw Frank Easter's castle. Without thinking, I ran to the big castle and climbed the wall on the ivy that ascended up to the arched window. 'Don't look down,' I mumbled to myself. I could hear the shouting of the policemen behind me. Finally, I made it to the window and dived through.

I ran as fast as I could, there was no time to waste. I saw a door and ran towards it, opened it and ran straight through. *Thump!* I ran into a tall man with a white beard and he fell right down the stairs and lay flat on the floor. Blood was rapidly pouring from his head. I knew I was going to faint by my eyesight slowly fading away . . .

I woke up in jail.

Paul Connell (11)
Willerby Carr Lane Junior School

ALIEN PROBLEM!

'Dad, there's an alien spaceship in the backyard,' Jim quivered.

'Don't be silly Jim, it's probably just a lamp post,' said Dad.

'No, really,' Jim said frantically.

Knowing something was up, Dad peered through the door. There in front of him was a sight he had never seen before - a spaceship. An alien slithered out, with fangs like chainsaws and ears, mouldy and long . . .

'Fetch the water gun,' Dad said.

Jim came down clutching the water gun. He was one on one with the alien.

Here goes nothing, Dad thought. But there was one thing wrong, the gun didn't work. Dad was torn apart like a shark eating a piece of meat. In this event, the spaceship hovered away out of sight. Dad suffered a lot of cuts and bruises and he was unconscious for a day, until he awoke in hospital. 'Where am I?' Dad said.

Later that day, Dad came home and cut the burnt and scorched grass where the spaceship had landed, and there on the ground was a letter. He read, *'We will be back . . .'*

Jack Gilson (10)
Willerby Carr Lane Junior School

A DAY IN THE LIFE OF MIA THERMOPOLIS

7.30
Wake up

7.50
Get out of bed. Breakfast. Mmmm . . . strawberries and cream. Yum!

8.00
Take out the trash.

8.45
Meet Lilly, my best friend, on the way to school.

8.55
Arrive at school, much to the delight of Lana Weinberger (cheerleader and bully) who I can never stick up to. OK, so I did stick up to her the other day. I smashed in her mobile, which is ultra hip (don't ask why).

9.00
Biology. Me and Kenny, my bio partner and boyfriend, are working on an ant assignment. I soooo do not love Kenny. I love my best friend's brother, Michael Moscovitz (He is so *buff!*). He soooo does not love me.

10.30
Algebra. *I hate algebra!* Even though my algebra teacher is my stepdad and my mum's having his baby, that doesn't mean I like algebra!

12.00
Lunch - *awful!* Lana is tormenting about only coming third in America's Favourite Royals competition. Because, by the way, *I'm Princess of Genovia!* Argh! *I hate it.*

1.00
English (boring club!) English is sooo *boring!* We have to write an essay on modern poetry.

2.30

G & T (Gifted and Talented) We do nothing in G & T because our teachers are always in the teachers' lounge, so I sit and stare at Michael all lesson. He's so cute!

3.30

Princess lessons with Grandmere are always dreadful! Grandmere teaches me to be princess-like.

5.00

Feed Fat Louie (my cat).

5.30

Dinner. Order a margharita pizza for tea. I'm vegetarian.

6.30

Instant message from Lilly about Greenpeace project.

8.00

Watch 'Baywatch'.

9.00

Go to bed, I'm sooo tired!

Jordan Rogers (11)
Willerby Carr Lane Junior School

WRITTEN IN BLOOD

'That movie was great!' exclaimed Tom excitedly.

'Yeah, shame about the party though, it's Hallowe'en, it's supposed to be about freaking people out. It's not exactly something I'd call scary!' Ellie disappointedly remarked.

Tom began to get an anxious feeling as they tiptoed closer and closer towards Tom's gloomy, dark house. Tom's house was totally dark, all the lights were switched off, which was very unusual as it is always very well lit and is a happy house. Finally he reached his front door, he twisted and turned the handle, but the door wouldn't open. His parents had been in earlier and had not planned on going out. He smashed the door open with a *wish-wash* karate kick. *Bang!* Blood droplets all around. Has it rained blood?

Upstairs, everything was a mess. The whole world spinning as he made his way warily down the stairs, trembling, shuffling into the kitchen and right before his eyes lay a smudged blood mark, and there in his family's blood was written: 'Your Hallowe'en has come true'. A blood trail led into the garden, but as he reached to open the door again, he realised it was locked. After that, he couldn't take much more. He leapt into the garden and there they stood, stone graves of every person in his family. And next to them laid the bodies.

'Ellie, is this a dream, no actually a really bad nightmare?' Tom wearily uttered.

'No Tom, it's not a dream, it's not a nightmare. It's real.'

There was deadly silence.

Some time later, Ellie suggested to call the police, but he couldn't face them. He was left with no family. On his own forever. Who would do such a terrible thing? Why? Why him?

Amy Cook (11)
Willerby Carr Lane Junior School

A Day In The Life Of Queen Victoria

12th February 1884

Today was a loathsome day. Of all days, today was most unpleasant.

A new servant arrived yesterday. This morning, in my royal bedchamber, she insulted my black clothes. Well, what I mean is that it is such a repulsive, unladylike thing to do. Tomorrow I will make her work an extra hour.

Later that day, I went out to open a new hospital. On the journey back, a man jumped from behind a bush and aimed a gun at my head. *Shoot!* Luckily for me, it missed. The man went red and ran off. Not very manly at all.

A couple of hours went by and I went to the grand ballroom to see some humorous entertainers. Basically, they fell over a lot. I was not amused by this nonsense of behaviour and ordered them never to step a foot in my palace again.

I have just found out that the servant that insulted me had been sacked from her first job because she forgot to iron the master's newspaper and gave cheek to the mistress. The court thought this was funny, but again, I was not amused.

Aliss Oxley (11)
Willerby Carr Lane Junior School

GHOST YARD

'I know what we can do,' shouted Lee anxiously, 'my friend told me about a haunted graveyard called Ghost Yard. It's only up the road.'
'Are you sure it's safe? I mean I know we've been bored to death for the last hour, but I don't like the sound of it.' Tina had long black hair and green eyes. She was very persistent. Lee, her brother, loves to go on what he calls adventures.
'No, it probably won't be safe, but that's the fun of it.'
Tina and Lee headed down the lane to the ghost yard!

When they got there, Tina's mouth dropped. Lee, on the other hand, smiled like a Cheshire cat at the adventure they were about to have. Lee opened the huge gate which squeaked loudly. They were in the ghost yard.

Tina followed through. By then it had started to get dark. Lee carried on walking. He came up to a large shed that was worn and battered.
'Don't even think about it. I'm not going in there.'
'You don't have to go, but I am.'
As Lee crept in the old shed, Tina heard howling whistles. *Argh!* He ran out of the shed. Tina screamed. They raced back through the ghost yard and through the squeaky gate. Tina turned around to see something chasing them, with a white face and a knife in its hand. They kept on running. Lee and Tina finally got back to their house.
'I am never going anywhere with you again,' bawled Tina.
'And I'm never going there again,' replied Lee.

Chloe Wade (11)
Willerby Carr Lane Junior School

THE GHOSTLY LANE

It was a dark, cold night and Harry was walking home down the creepy lane. It was light when he set off at about 4pm, but as he walked down the lane, he realised that the darkness was crawling across the sky, and as black clouds rolled across the moon, Harry began to get scared.

Suddenly, he heard a rustling noise coming from a small bush. Then there was the same noise coming from a large pine tree. Harry backed away. Out of nowhere, a huge black shadow leapt across the tarmac lane. Harry ran. But the further he ran, the beasts seemed to get faster and they started gaining speed. Harry ran into the trees in an attempt to escape from the beasts. He turned round, to look forward at a field of - gravestones!

Suddenly, the ground started to wobble and Harry's legs had already disappeared. Then after five minutes, he fell straight through the floor. There was an underground cavern, but it was like an everlasting tunnel. He started to run again, but a huge baboon held up a knife. Harry yelled, then he opened his eyes and his mum was leaning over him. Harry looked surprised. 'I suppose it was only a dream,' he said.

Lauren Drasdo (11)
Willerby Carr Lane Junior School

FALSE TEETH

I was only about four years old at the time, and it was my first time at a sleepover.

'See you later then,' said my mum, 'and don't forget to be good for Granny when she picks you up tomorrow.'

'I'm going to a restaurant tomorrow,' I said to my friend Jade.

'Cool,' she answered. 'I wish I could go with you.'

'Sorry,' I said, 'but it's a lot of pennies.'

We were allowed to stay up till half-eight, which we thought was really cool.

The next morning, My granny came to pick me up in her clunky old green mini.

'We're going to the restaurant straight away,' croaked Granny, 'so we won't be late for lunch.'

Eventually we reached the fish restaurant on the corner of Volage Court. My grandad was sat on table 16. He had already ordered lunch. He and Granny were having mussels and I was having fish fingers. Just as a man was serving my dinner, my granny took out a hanky and coughed her teeth into it (they were false teeth, of course). I stared at her in amazement, and she smiled at me, looking like a witch without her teeth.

After Granny and Grandad had taken me home, teatime came round quickly. My mum put my pasta in front of me. I was just about to start eating, when I remembered what Granny had done. I took out my hanky and began coughing into it. My mum looked at me.

'What's wrong, Claire?' she asked.

And I replied, 'I'm trying to get my teeth out - like Granny does.'

Charlotte Grimbleby (10)
Willerby Carr Lane Junior School

THE ALIENS ARE COMING!

No one believes me, but I promise it's true. It all happened yesterday, it was a full moon and the stars were bright. So I decided to look out of my bedroom window. There it was, red and flashing, bright and shiny.

'Mum, Mum,' I screeched, 'a spaceship.'
'Don't be so ridiculous Jake, you're going bananas,' she laughed.
'It's true,' I growled, slamming my door violently.
Even my best friend Charlie wouldn't believe me or even my little sister Ellen and she's only 7. *I've gone mad,* I thought to myself. Right, I'll prove it's true. I'll take a photograph! Then someone will have to believe me.

So I sat there staring - nothing! Forty-five minutes and nothing. Until all of a sudden there it was, spinning. Its red lights like fiery eyes and its shiny body like armour. I grabbed my camera. *Click!* There, perfect. I stood staring patiently, waiting for my picture to focus. I had proof. Surely someone would believe me now, as the picture began to become clearer. There it was in the night sky, but the spaceship was just a big blur. I was doomed, well and truly doomed! Now no one would realise I was right. How can I prove that the aliens are coming?

Charlotte Levy (11)
Willerby Carr Lane Junior School

THE FUNNY SLEEPOVER

Hi. I'm Cally. I'm 11 years old. My friend Hannah is also 11 but a bit younger. We're having a sleepover tonight at my house and Hannah is here now. 'Shall we set up the sofa?'
'OK then.'

It was 11 o'clock by the time we'd had a snack and brushed our teeth. Hannah went on one sofa and I went on the other. Hannah fell asleep straight away then I went to sleep a moment after. My brother started sleep-walking and came into the room making motorbike noises because he loves motorbikes and he has his own CR80. He burst into the room.
Hannah screamed, 'Who's that?'
'Don't worry, it's only my brother, he sleep-walks.'
'Oh.' We both started laughing till we were in stitches.
He went back to bed and we fell asleep.

The next morning, me and Hannah had Weetabix for breakfast. We got changed and went on my trampoline, then took turns on my electric scooter that has a horn, indicators and also headlights. I can go up to 15 miles per hour on full charge.

Later in the day Hannah said, 'Why is your brother so scary when he sleeps?'
'I don't know, but let's go tell him how stupid he's been,' said Hannah giggling.

Cally Beech (11)
Willerby Carr Lane Junior School

THE GHOST SHIP!

One fine night in Whitby, Timothy Tailor was aboard a ship. Then suddenly the weather became wet and stormy, the air became cold and the hairs on the back of his neck stood up. Tailor quickly anchored his ship to the seabed and ran to the bow. He took out his binoculars and looked into the distance.

He could see a faint outline of a ship, it looked like a white or grey colour. But he couldn't really see. Suddenly the ship took a sharp turn towards Tailor. He ran for the anchor, pulled and pulled, but the anchor must have been stuck on a rock! The boat was getting closer and closer and Tailor was getting more scared by the second. The boat shook as the ship crashed into the bow side of Tailor's ship.

Tailor lay shocked on the floor. A tall, white figure stood in front of him. Suddenly Tailor fell unconscious. The figure picked him up and laid him on his ship. Then they sailed away into the distance.

A few days later Tailor's ship was found still anchored to the seabed. His wife thought he had fallen overboard and drowned. His workmates said he was depressed and could have killed himself. But no one really knows what happened to Timothy Tailor!

Emma Norton (11)
Willerby Carr Lane Junior School

WHO'S THERE?

'Hannah,' whispered Charlotte, quivering.
'What do you want?' moaned Hannah, turning over in bed.
'I think someone's downstairs . . .'
Suddenly there was a huge *thud* and a sound of breaking glass.
Hannah jumped up and slowly they crept towards the staircase,
Charlotte close behind her.

It was midnight and the two sisters on Brightly Road were creeping
down the stairs. When they reached the bottom, Hannah gasped. She
was shocked at such a terrible mess! As they entered the kitchen, a tall,
yet dark-looking creature stood before them. Something was sharp and
glistening in its hand. The girls screamed. All of a sudden the light
flickered . . .
'Oh what a relief,' said Charlotte.
It was Cally, their younger sister!

Sarah Boyce (11)
Willerby Carr Lane Junior School

THE BLACK HOLE

I walked into the living room. As I grabbed the remote for the TV I heard a strange howling noise and it seemed to be coming from the television. The noise repeated around the room as I started to feel like something was happening. It got louder and louder as the weather turned from sun to rain.

I sat on the sofa in silence as a black hole reached out to my weak feet and I tried to stop it. It really started to push me in, but I clung on to the sofa as the hole sucked me in harder by the second. Charlie and James walked into the room with grins on their faces.
'Don't just stand there you idiots,' I yelled as I got sucked in.

Suddenly the hole got worse as Charlie and James tried to help. Amazingly I got out of the hole, but Charlie and James died.
'No,' I shouted in tears as I nearly got pushed back in.

Joe Glenton (11)
Willerby Carr Lane Junior School

THE DARE GAME

Sarah, Tom, Hannah, Lee, Cally and Joel were playing the dare game when Sarah dared Lee to kiss Cally. He shook and his faced dropped - he felt very scared. Would he succeed? Ten minutes later the dare began.

Quickly Lee pecked Cally on the cheek. He did it, he was successful, but there was one tiny problem, a teacher was watching. She ran telling the headmistress straight away. When play time had ended there was a knock on the door.
'Could I have Lee please?'
'Certainly,' said Mrs Rhodes.
'You know what this is about don't you?'
'Yes, the dare game.'
'I don't want you kissing girls in my school. What you do in your own time is not up to me, so make sure it doesn't happen again,' yelled Mrs Gilson.

Lee came back into the classroom shaking. 'I'm not playing that game again,' he said.

Lee Hairsine (11)
Willerby Carr Lane Junior School

THE INVADERS

Crash, bang!
'What was that?' screamed Mum.
'I don't know,' said Dad.
Jimmy came running through, 'Dad, go and find out what the noise is,' ordered Jimmy.
'Okay.'
Dad went into the kitchen . . . *zap!*
'Argh!' screamed Mum and Jimmy.
Next Mum went to investigate. She slowly, quietly walked into the kitchen . . . *zap!*
'Argh!' screamed Jimmy. He looked out of the window and saw the spaceship setting off. He jumped out of the window landing in a pile of glass. He got up and found the best thing he could (a hose reel) and switched it on, pointing it at the engine. The spaceship started to stutter and stall and finally crashed.

Jimmy went inside, but was surrounded by aliens. He pushed the *No Gravity* button. Suddenly everybody was floating in mid-air. He swam towards Mum and Dad and got them out!

That night they had a party and celebrated not being abducted by aliens. Jimmy though was disappointed because he thought he was a hero.

Steven Pye (11)
Willerby Carr Lane Junior School

THE BLACK SKULL

'What's happening?' squealed Sam.

'Don't ask me,' mumbled Peter.

The black-skulled skeletons were pounding, hitting the ground to get out of their dirty, smelly coffins and graves.

All of the skeletons were moving forward, lumping and lashing the thin air. Sam and Peter picked up some spades. They were both thumping and hammering the skeletons, but it was no use, they were too strong.

The boys, Sam and Peter, both ran in separate directions, but they were both soon surrounded. The skeletons were closing in. They barged through the weak point of the skeletons and ran into a wooden hut. They were safe, or they thought they were.

Bang! Bang! The skeletons were trying to push the wooden hut down. They were smashing all the glass windows. Peter pulled off the black skull that was on the skeleton that was climbing in. Suddenly the skeleton fell to the ground. All of them did.

Sam and Peter heard a crack as the hut fell down. They woke up. They were in the middle of their bedroom. They couldn't move. They were too scared, but then they realised it was just a dream - until they saw the *black skull*.

Lewis Heald (10)
Willerby Carr Lane Junior School

BALLOON DISASTER!

'See you later, have a good time,' said Mum while waving her arms frantically.

'Let's go,' smiled Steven.

'I'm not sure,' whispered Bobby.

'I just can't believe we're going on a hot air balloon finally - we're going to have a great time.'

'Off we go,' shouted Bobby.

The view's amazing.'

'I can't see,' said Bobby reaching up.

'I'll lift you, 1, 2, 3, up.'

'Help!' shouted Bobby.

He had fallen over the side.

Steven quickly grabbed the help box and threw a rope down.

'Grab onto it, quick,' screamed Steven. He pulled Bobby up into safety.

'Phew, I never want to see the ground again,' said Bobby, whilst wiping the sweat off his head.

'Let's land now,' smiled Steven.

'There's Mum, don't tell her about what's happened. Let's keep it a secret between you and me.'

'Hi you two,' said Mum. 'Have you had a good time?'

'Definitely,' they chorused.

'Well, you'll have to go again,' she said.

Bobby's eyes widened in fear.

Jessica Lees (10)
Willerby Carr Lane Junior School

VAMPIRE NIGHT

It was the middle of the night at my house. I couldn't sleep, my sister was snoring. She stopped. It was too quiet - something was up. I went to see Kirsty, she was *gone*. Where was she? I went to tell Mum and Dad, but they were gone too. I heard a noise coming from outside.

Outside there were four dark figures standing at the end of the garden. I recognised three of them, but the other one I didn't. Just then they ran at me. I saw another figure.
'I'm dead,' I said.
'No you're not,' said the figure.

He jumped down.
'Blade!' I mumbled under my breath. He staked one figure, then another. Finally he faced the leader. *Stab*, he was dead.
'Your mum, dad and Kirsty are in the basement,' said Blade and then he was gone!

Steven Norris (10)
Willerby Carr Lane Junior School

DRESSED IN BLACK

Bang, crash, rip! Suddenly I woke up, there were noises downstairs, but I couldn't tell what they were.

So I got out of bed and slowly walked towards the top of the stairs.
'Get back to bed Laura!' shouted Mum. I stayed where I was. I carried on going downstairs because Mum had gone back to sleep. I glanced at the room, then I saw black mud all over, the curtains were ripped, pans were on the floor and the cupboards were open. I was scared.

Then I saw a shadow on the wall. I walked round the corner and there stood right in front of me was a man dressed in a black suit with an axe. I screamed and ran. He chased after me all round the house, smashing and breaking more things. I ran out the house. He hit my back with the axe. I fell to the floor and he ran away.

The next thing I remember was the noise of the ambulance. I woke up and I looked around. All my family were standing around me. I was in hospital.

Josie Long (11)
Willerby Carr Lane Junior School

FOREST FRIGHT

One day Brian and Vikki, two best friends, went walking together in a forest. They knew this forest well, but chose a path that they had never been down before and thought they would go for a longer walk. They did not expect to get lost on this path.

As they set off for their walk, they did not realise that two red eyes were following them. The path led them deep into the heart of the forest. Still the red eyes were following. It was only then that they noticed the red eyes. They looked at each other and ran for their lives, screaming as they went.

They ran and ran until they were outside of the forest. They heard a growl, but the creature did not appear to be there. They never went near the forest again.

Jemma Brindle (10)
Willerby Carr Lane Junior School

THURSDAY THE 12TH

'Come on, nearly there,' said Lizzie.
'Why are we doing this?' replied Stephanie.
'Because.'
'Because what?'
'Because if you don't I'll get you grounded for a year.'
'Why?'
'Because . . . okay!'
'Yes.'

Suddenly in the distance a twig snapped and Stephanie started to wonder if the rumour was true? They waited until day came to go and see if there were any footprints of the someone or something that was following them.

The next day Lizzie realised that it was Friday the 13th and she knew that whatever was following them would be back.

'Stephanie, I can feel warm air down my neck.'
Suddenly they turned around to find that the person or thing that was following them was only their best friend Jessica.

Victoria Waymark (10)
Willerby Carr Lane Junior School

ERICK BONJOVIE

The name is Erick, Erick BonJovie. I'm the future James Bond. I work like him, but don't live like him. This is the story of the missing sock.

It all started one misty Friday night. Well, actually it was the steam from the shower. But all the same . . . I clambered out of the shower, got dry and started to get dressed. But just then I realised one of my socks was missing. I decided to look for it. I searched behind the wash basket and in the toilet. I ran down to the graveyard, strange things always happen there.

I arrived there and was walking through the gates. But just then I saw something. It was cloaked in black and there was now an awful smell in the air so I kicked the thing and grabbed my sock. As I ran away I thought, *maybe I'll be a new Scooby-Doo instead.*

I strolled along the street triumphant. Just then all my hopes sank. I felt a slimy hand on my shoulder. I slowly turned my head. A twisted face looked at me through the shadows of a hood. Slowly it lowered its cloak to reveal a bald, green head, with two heartless eyes. I backed off and curled up in a corner, throwing the sock. But then it spoke, 'I don't want that, I just brought your keys.' And with that it vanished.

Chris Rutty (11)
Willerby Carr Lane Junior School

HORROR LAND

Andy and Dino were best friends. They had been since Year 1. They walked up the stone steps to the entrance of Horror Land. They watched a Punch and Judy show with special guest Dracula. Next they saw costume makers and asked for skeleton costumes - they also bought pretend axes.

After a long time they noticed the people who went on the horror coaster came out very pale. Andy and Dino got on for the ride of their lives - literally. The ride set off. Bats flew above them. Some doors opened and a skeleton fell from high up. It landed on someone behind them. Water sprayed in their faces. Some giant skeletons started riding bikes. Suddenly one of the skeletons punched one of the passengers behind Andy and Dino, killing him.

By this time Andy and Dino were very scared. Andy jumped out of the carriage and ran towards the door. Suddenly he heard a scream. Dino was on the floor dead. Andy continued to run, he reached the door and pushed it open. Suddenly everything stopped. All the staff started to change shape. Soon they were all monsters.

The pretend axe began to glow, soon it became very heavy. The axe stopped glowing and became a proper axe. Andy attacked the monsters one by one. Finally he reached the gate. He turned around only to see the ghost of Dino stab him . . .

Adam Stephenson (10)
Willerby Carr Lane Junior School

ESCAPE FROM BRINTLY'S SCHOOL

As Miss Cringe walked briskly down the corridor, Ryan was determined to escape. Three months detention and all he'd done was put a rubber spider in a cup of tea belonging to Mr Ghastly, who just happened to suffer from arachnaphobia.

'Miss Cringe, Miss Cringe,' he heard. That meant only one thing, Alex Christmas, although there was nothing Christmassy about him.
'Naughty, naughty,' Alex cackled devilishly, 'out of your dormitory after 9 o'clock.'
'And what are you doing here then?' replied Ryan.
'Helping me on night patrol.'
Ryan swallowed, it was Mrs Brintly . . . she was the owner of the school and the strictest teacher. 'Four months detention Ryan Smith,' she squawked.

He had an escape plan; he just needed the right moment. He couldn't stand another day there. He packed his bag and made a rope from bed sheets. After tying the rope to the bedstead, he grabbed the other end and leapt out of the window.

Mrs Brintly had always said that someone would try to escape. Therefore she had a barbed wire fence fitted around the school. That was not enough to stop Ryan; he had *borrowed* a shovel from the caretaker. He tunnelled under the fence, swallowing just one earthworm before he scrambled through to the other side.

Ryan ran to the nearby train station and jumped onto a train - a train to Bradford, his home town! The train trundled through the cold night; he was so hungry that he wished he had brought another worm! But he arrived home the next day tired, hungry but *free!*

Joseph Griffiths (10)
Willerby Carr Lane Junior School

COLLEGE CATASTROPHE

'Would you then?' asked Fabio.
Dexter didn't reply. He was shocked, gobsmacked, his whole body was numb. Finally he answered, 'Me? I'd love to.'
Dexter had just been invested into the most magnificent college. He couldn't believe it. Eyeballs boggling, mind boiling with excitement.
'Well, I'll see you in September,' cried Fabio (headmaster of Sandstone College). Fabio exited Dexter's house and rode off in his flash limousine.

It was Monday 16th September, first day of college. Dexter waved to his mum - who was in tears - whilst he stood at the grand doorway of Sandstone College. He was as nervous as he was well-dressed. Shakily he pushed the door open, stepped inside and gasped. The view was amazing! Walls with portraits of distinguished people and diplomas. Vast rugs covered the ruby-coloured carpet.

After a couple of days Dexter had one desire and one friend. His friend was a gawky no one called Arnold. His desire was to be in a tough gang - *Greg's Gang*. Firstly they had to execute two devious missions.

Arnold explained both missions to Dexter. He whispered, 'You steal the confiscated stink bombs, then I'll crawl through the air vents leading to the cafeteria, put the air vent into reverse and let them off.'

The second mission was to burn the year tests, but Clyde (the snitch) saw them plotting it and told Fabio.
'I can explain,' cried Dexter.
'No need to, I know everything thanks to Clyde. You are both in extreme trouble and your parents will be informed!'

Matthew Adamson (11)
Willerby Carr Lane Junior School

SQUEAKY'S WISH

Once upon a time there was a dog, a cat and a mouse. None of them liked each other. As you know, mice they really, really, really like cheese so because the owners have gone on holiday for seven days and the only thing they buy is cheese, the mouse will be having the time of his life.

'Stop, can we get to the story now?'

'Fine!'

Squeak, squeak!

Miaow, miaow!

Woof, woof!

That is the sound of a dog, cat and mouse chase. I'm the narrator and I can't take it . . . *pant* . . . *pant* . . . *pant.*

Anyway, one very special day (Squeaky's birthday party) which every one of Squeaky's family was invited. He was nibbling on a piece of cheesecake when . . . he bit something hard, he spat it out and it started to say, 'Squeak, squeak, squeak!' That means: you have three wishes.

'*Three wishes*, ooh cool, I'm going all right? To choose my wishes.'

'Yes!'

'Bye-bye!'

As soon as Squeaky got out, *snap.* Miaowy ate poor little Squeaky. Very luckily Squeaky had his pneumatic drill and drilled Miaowy's teeth and climbed out. The mouse ran as hard as he could until his tiny legs couldn't run any further. He took shelter in the cheese on the table.

Suddenly the *thing* said, 'Two wishes.' Squeaky gasped and looked outside. The dog disappeared.

'I wish the cat disappeared and I can have a show in Las Vegas.'

Bang!

'Las Vegas, here I come!'

Tom Robertson (10)

Willerby Carr Lane Junior School

DON'T OPEN THAT BIN!

A boy lived in Pennsylvania at 12 Unlucky Street. He was a monster-eating chocolate fan who ate one trillion bars of chocolate every week. His name was Snackula. This time when he went to get a chocolate bar there was none left so he went to the shops. He bought some. After he'd eaten them all he had to clean up all the wrappers, filling up all of his 79,000 rooms. He had to clean it all up before his mum came home. He ran up and down all the stairs and when he came to the last wrapper he put it in the bin. Suddenly the bin got hold of his arm and bit it off.

The next day when his friend came he went to the 666 kitchen and he saw his friend on the floor and on the wall in blood it said, 'Don't open this bin again or you'll be my next victim!' That boy was never to be seen again.

Nathan Dennison (11)
Willerby Carr Lane Junior School

LIFT-OFF FAILS!

'5, 4, 3, 2, 1, lift-off,' yelled Louis the take-off commander.

'How come we're moving downwards then?' replied Joe and Moe the spacemen.

'You were off the ground a minute ago,' Louis said in a puzzled way.

'Oh no, we're going to crash!'

Bang, clang, thud.

At that moment the space rocket (Apollo XIII) burst into flames.

'I'm a spaceman,' shouted Joe.

'Get me out of here!' panicked Moe.

'I can't do anything, I'm miles away from you. You'll have to do it all yourselves.'

Both Moe and Joe knew that this was a matter of life and death. When the two men had taken their seatbelts off they could feel the heat burning their bodies.

'At last,' Joe sighed, 'fresh air.'

Joe and Moe knew that they had to run because the spacecraft was gonna blow!

Alex Easter (11)
Willerby Carr Lane Junior School

THE DAY AND LIFE OF A HOLIDAYMAKER!

I was in a water park (called Sea World) with my mum and dad. We fed some dolphins when we saw a sign up for the Shamu Show. It was fantastic the last time we saw it, all those excellent stunts they did. My mum and dad thought it was good as well when they went. So we decided to see it again.

We got front seats, but there was just one thing we had forgotten . . . the show had started and after only ten seconds we were soaked. They also did a little trick on us.

Once it was over we went to a restaurant. The food was delicious, I had spaghetti Bolognese with meatballs and garlic bread and a tutti-frutti cocktail to wash it down and keep me chilled from the lovely hot weather.

A while later we went for a luxurious swim in the Sealife ocean. After that we finished our swim and went back to the hotel. For tea we had a roast dinner with turkey and a shandy. Then we watched a film called *Labyrinth*, it was a bit awkward, but still good and still quite funny.

Finally, I had a delightful, mouth-watering cup of chocolate expresso and went to bed.

Kathryn Lawrie (11)
Willerby Carr Lane Junior School

SCHOOL WITH A GHOUL!

'It has been found that Sir Scaredric's School which burnt down in the 1800s is haunted.'

'That reporter's gone bonkers,' Jamie's dad said, switching off the TV and shaking his bald head grumpily. Later that night Jamie called his mate Kat and asked her if she'd seen the news.

'Well, that's a ridiculous question. What do you think Jamie?' she asked him.

'Of, of course,' he replied. Her parents are only addicted to it why shouldn't I know?

They had planned to meet outside the gate on Friday night at midnight under the full moon. So they climbed over the gate and *bang,* Jamie had fallen face first over the gate. They slowly approached the old, burnt door of the school.

Clang! Went the door behind, then Jamie tried the door.

'It's locked,' he said.

'Let me try,' Kat said shakily. 'Oops!'

'What do you mean?' Jamie asked. He tried the handle, *clang, clang, bang.* The handle had fallen off and echoed around the hall.

Meanwhile, up in the old, crumbling staffroom Sir Scaredric croaked, 'We have company,' turning his half-burnt, mouldy head to My Lady Murder who was wearing a burnt dress and had long black hair with one eye.

Downstairs in the huge hall with burnt curtains and bones, the two children made their way up the crumbling stairs when . . . *crash*, they fell through a trapdoor and were picked up by two frightening zombies.

They found themselves in a room, tied to a chair with zombies closing in on them. They screamed. That was the last anyone ever head of them.

Lilly Ward (10)
Willerby Carr Lane Junior School

CHILLS AND CREEPS

'Come on, we are almost there,' shouted Steph.

'I'm coming, I'm not as fast as you,' replied Lizzie. 'Why are we coming here in the first place?' asked Lizzie.

'I heard my sister talking about it, she said something about someone being killed,' said Steph excitedly.

A wolf howled, they both jumped, then a roar of thunder.

'Come on,' said Steph again.

They reached a huge, black door. The windows were filled with cobwebs, as spiders tumbled from the walls. Then the door creaked open, they looked at each other then stepped into the darkness. The door slammed behind them. The darkness flooded the room.

'Steph,' trembled Lizzie, 'I don't like the dark.'

'I know, did you watch Buffy last night?' asked Steph.

'Yes, why?' replied Lizzie.

'Because she clapped her hands and . . .'

Clap! Clap!

'The light's come on,' said Steph wisely.

'*Wow!* How did you do that?' replied Lizzie.

Steph just tapped her nose.

As Steph walked round proudly, she saw something, a puddle, a blood puddle. 'Lizzie?' said Steph trying not to make a lot of noise. 'Lizzie?' she said again.

She was gone. Steph walked up to the puddle - it was fresh and leading to a bookshelf. She pulled all the books off the shelf, then the shelf swung open. There sat Lizzie bleeding, but still alive. She picked her up and carried her home.

Stephanie Steels (11)
Willerby Carr Lane Junior School

THE CLOCK

It was my 12th birthday and my uncle had given me a clock with tribal carvings on it. One week later the clock stopped. I changed the batteries, but it still didn't work. I even asked Bob next door what was wrong with it because he worked in a clock shop, but even he didn't know. What was wrong with the clock?

Suddenly the clock burst into a ball of multicoloured light. I was being pulled into a portal. I tried to resist, but it was just too strong. I flew around a sparkling, spiralling, super swirling tunnel. I couldn't think of a word to describe the tunnel. I got further down the tunnel and realised there were other tunnels leading off with signs saying *3000AD*. I couldn't believe it, I was going forward in time!

When I got up I looked around. I was shocked! The whole planet was one big wasteland. There were no trees, no plants, no grass, no animals, nothing. The air was so polluted I could hardly breathe. I started to explore. The air was completely covered in smog and dust. The only thing that was visible was litter. The Earth was covered head to toe in litter!

I had a sudden thought. The clock had brought me here to show me what would happen to the world if we kept littering like we do now. So next time you are about to throw litter, think what would happen to the Earth in just a short amount of time.

Adam Thompson (10)
Willerby Carr Lane Junior School

BUMP! BUMP!

Bump! Bump! The roof was drumming, thought Timmy as he lay in his over-sized cot. He was 3 years old and still wet his bed. In fact, he was wet right now. *Bump! Clang!* Someone had knocked over big Phil's drumkit in the room above the stairs (someone was in the loft messing with Timmy's big brother Phil's drums).

'Let's investigatey, likey Indianay Joney,' announced Timmy, as he crawled over the side of the cot onto his very expensive train set, breaking everything into tiny pieces.

'Ow! bot-bot hurties.' He wriggled over to the door and to the ladder which led to the room. *Ouch!* This was from upstairs. This had to be investigated. The ladder looked so tall, but brave Timmy had a job to do. It must have taken him at least two hours to even attempt to climb the ladder, which would have given the burglar (who he was) time to go to the moon and back. The burglar ran down the ladder at the sound of Timmy letting off wind, until he met the culprit of the pump, Timmy.

'Stop in the namey of the law, Sonny Jim,' demanded Timmy as he ran out from the bathroom.

Timmy's eyes began to flick to the thing the burglar was carrying. His teddy bear. 'Get off him,' demanded Timmy, running up onto the burglar and water hosing all over him. He dropped the bear and jumped out the window.

'You'll get it, kid!'

Ross Jennings (11)
Willerby Carr Lane Junior School

SCHOOL OF NIGHTMARES

'But I don't want to go,' commanded Kelly.

'Neither do I,' yelled Mark.

Kelly and Mark were trying to argue their way out of boarding school. They were both 11 but each had an uncontrollable attitude, so their parents had had enough. They didn't want their children growing up to be monsters.

So they gathered their stuff and got into the purple Jeep and headed for Deep Heart Boarding School in Deepershire. When they first arrived Kelly and Mark thought it was the haunted house out of Alton Towers, not a boarding school. Well, they were unfortunately wrong. Kelly and Mark grabbed their stuff out the boot and the Jeep sped away.

The gates were tall and covered in thick, black, wet paint. Smoke filled the air. The building was next to a graveyard. It was red with only two windows. Inside it was dull with not much light - all the pictures were covered in grey dust and there were over 556 rooms.

Kelly and Mark both looked for their rooms and unpacked to get ready for tea. When they arrived at the canteen everyone was in uniform and sat quietly drinking tea. Kelly and Mark looked around for a table and sat down. Three of the students came over and warned Kelly and Mark that scary things were about to happen at Deep Heart Boarding School. Mark and Kelly were about to say to each other to take no notice, but they realised that the school was kind of freaky anyway. So they decided to check the place out, but before they could reach the door the headmistress grabbed their arms and took them both to their rooms.

'Get to sleep now, breakfast is at 8 o'clock,' ordered the headmistress.

Mark and Kelly didn't bother arguing and got into bed. In the middle of the night they were both woken up by a loud banging sound. They could see shadows forming on the walls of the room and trees whistled with horror. Both of them started to panic. Sweat dripped from their faces. They saw a white figure in the distance, their hearts started to race. It disappeared. The white figure vanished. After a long discussion and fretting they eventually fell asleep.

The next morning at breakfast Kelly and Mark tried to find the three students that they had spoken to yesterday to try and find out more about it, but they had departed to visit their parents. They tried to find out some more information in the library, but there was nothing.

The next night the same shadows appeared and the white figure came again. They thought it was just their imagination till the ghost held up his knife!

Hannah Richardson (11)
Willerby Carr Lane Junior School

ALIENS, THEY WALK AMONG US

Nobody will believe me. Not even my own family. I was at my best friend's house and was having a perfectly good night until I went to get some food from the Chinese. Suddenly I heard a tree creak and a bright light appear from around the corner.

I walked towards it sticking as close to the wall as I could. I turned my head around the corner and couldn't believe what I saw. Two eight-foot figures were talking to each other in a strange dialect that I had never heard of. Green slime dripped and formed a large puddle that bubbled and fizzed every minute. They both walked towards me in a very egotistical manner. I ran as fast as I could away from these terrible creatures. But when I got to my friend's house they were gone. I kept knocking on the door, but there was no answer.

After that, the first thought that came to my mind was . . . *Get to the nearest phone booth and ring the police.* I picked up the phone, but the line was dead. I didn't know what to do.

Johnny Wilkinson (11)
Willerby Carr Lane Junior School

GHOST TREE

'It's Christmas,' yelped Phill as he ran down the stairs. He opened the living room door and screamed with horror, there was a skeleton lying on the Christmas tree with a skull, arms and legs. It slowly lifted itself up, but it was stuck to the tree. Like a ghost tree it chased Phill round and round.

'Open a pressie little boy.'

'Argh!' Phill screamed. He grabbed presents, throwing them at the freaky figure.

'I'm your new Santa,' the psycho coldly exclaimed.

'Argh,' Phill suddenly woke up, it was just a dream.

He looked out of the window, the beautiful crystals of snow were falling down, 'It's Christmas, Mum, Dad, it's Christmas.'

Phill ran downstairs, his presents were in the kitchen, as soon as he had eaten his Christmas dinner he went in the living room. He had forgotten about his horrible dream, but there on the top of the Christmas tree was the skull of the ghost. Phil screamed.

Mum and Dad ran into the room, 'What is it?'

'Look!' shouted Phill.

'Argh!' they yelped.

'I will kill you!'

'This is the worst Christmas ever,' Dad sobbed.

With an instant flash the skull split into hundreds of tiny bits and suddenly Mum, Dad and Phill lay dead on the ground.

Alex Fox (11)
Willerby Carr Lane Junior School

GHOST HOUSE

I was lost in the middle of a forest, the only thing I could see were trees and more trees, it was really scary. I walked along the big, bushy leaves and grass. I found a small house covered in vines. *I was saved.*

I walked in, it was dark, too dark, every so often I felt a breeze, a cold one, a bad one. I walked into a room there were lots of spiders' webs and spiders.

I ran upstairs, I saw lots of white figures bobbing and turning. It was freaky. I ran back down the stairs and out of the door, slamming it behind me. I thought, *Maybe I could be a detective and solve the mystery.* I went inside and into all the rooms downstairs and found nothing but a gory, dead man.

I went upstairs and saw the ghosts again. I wasn't scared at all, I acted like a strong man (but I was weak really). I went in one room, there was a bed, a chair, a mirror (which I could only just see myself through) and a cabinet.

The next room was a tiny room, it had just enough room to fit a bed in. It had a wardrobe as well that could only just fit in. I came to the final room, it was a huge room. It had loads more room in it.
'Boo!'

Greg Lound (10)
Willerby Carr Lane Junior School

THE BEE

One day Romer (Dad), Marge (Mum), Lisa (Sister) and Bart (Me) were at a garage sale. We were all looking around. Dad bought two teleporters for 36p. We brought them home and Dad did a few tests. He put one of them upstairs and the other downstairs. He walked into the upstairs one and ended up downstairs.

Afterwards he went to New Zealand for a holiday. He won £1 million. He took the teleporter so he could get a beer from the fridge at home. He started building more and more teleporters, but Marge thought he was going nuts again. So she decided to sit him down and talk to him, but he was yapping on about hot dogs.

So Marge went to the Fast 'E' Mart to get him some hot dog-flavoured cigars. Romer was puffing on his cigars whilst Marge was yapping on about the teleporters being removed.

Anyway, I was messing around with it. I went into one and came out the other with my head and a bee's body. I didn't realise a bee had got mixed into my DNA. I was shouting, 'Help, help!' Nobody could hear me. It came out a sort of wasp noise. Was I doomed or was it a dream? *Argh . . . noooo . . . splat!*

Matthew Fewster (10)
Willerby Carr Lane Junior School

AGENT 006.5291748

Agent 006.5291748 - Scott - heard noises downstairs, he went to look
out of the window and saw . . .

'Oh my God!' Scott said. 'Dr Wannabe Evil's next door, my worst
nightmare!'
Ping pong! The doorbell rang, Scott went to open the door.
'Hello Scott, we meet again,' said my next-door neighbour. 'Would you
like to come to my barbecue?'
'Yeah, cheers,' said Scott.
'OK then, I'm sure it will be death-defying,' he said, creepily as he put
his little finger to his mouth.

Scott, with his protection, a 9mm automatic, walked next door. A waiter
came up to him and offered him a hot dog. He refused.

About half an hour later, people started dying.
'Dr Wannabe Evil, you did this!' He got out his gun and shot him five
times in the head. 'Why aren't you dying?'
'I don't know, it's just a story,' said Dr Wannabe Evil. 'Maybe the
writer wants me to live on. Viva the writer!'
'Well, I'm not going to let you!' He leapt onto Dr Wannabe and pushed
him into pool.
'We'll meet again!' said Dr Wannabe Evil, as he climbed out of the
pool and into the shed. He pressed a button and it blasted off into space.

David Cartlich (11)
Willerby Carr Lane Junior School

THE STUPID BULLY

'Leave me along, Jordan,' Charlotte yelled, as Jordan grabbed for her dinner money.

Charlotte was the best at maths, best at science, best at English and best at getting bullied. Jordan was not very good at much, apart from fighting. She was jealous of Charlotte. Jordan loved to bully Charlotte.

Charlotte was starting to fight back. She tried everything in her power to overcome Jordan, but Jordan was too good.

One day Charlotte was walking down the hallway in school, when a foot stuck out and Charlotte tripped over it. She stood up and looked Jordan in the eyes. As hard as she could, Charlotte punched Jordan in the face. Jordan screamed as loud as she could and never went near Charlotte again.

Penny Chapman (11)
Willerby Carr Lane Junior School

A Fright To Remember

Tom was a 12-year-old boy. He loved to go on adventures. He also got himself into serious trouble when he thought he had done good.

One boring day he was coming home from a normal (normal for him anyway) day at school, when he went past Shiverdown Graveyard. He suddenly heard a ghostly sound coming from the murky depths of the shopping market of dead bodies.
'Crikey!' Tom cried.
He ran as fast as he could to the comfort of his own home. Later he thought he would go and find out what that freaky noise was.

Secretly, he sneaked out and made his way into the murkiness of the graveyard. Slowly, he walked across into the centre of the graveyard. By accident he stood on a twig which cracked. With that, everything seemed to come alive.

The wind whistled as it followed Tom. Tom's eyes could only see a small way through the gathering mist. He fell over a large pile of leaves and landed in a musky pile of dirt, left over from the diggings of a burial. He brought himself to an upright position. A leaf moved from beneath his foot and a large barn owl flew from a nearby tree. He screamed and hid behind a remembrance stone.

It appeared to him that there were shadows forming in the skies above. Almost as suddenly as it came, everything went silent. From behind eight gravestones emerged eight dead, mouldy zombies. He stepped backwards and fell over a brick. The zombies came closer and closer. Tom put his hand to his frightened face. What was going to happen to him? He would never know.

Alex Holt (11)
Willerby Carr Lane Junior School

SWAPPING LIVES

'Jack, get ready for school, it's your first day remember?'
Jack is a young boy aged 11. Skinny, weak, vacant expression, he is the main character in the story.
'Jack, I said get ready!' bellowed Mum.
'OK. Let me finish my breakfast,' he whined.

As he made his way to his new school, he came across a shop with Voodoo R Us on the top. He had half an hour to get to school and he could not help himself, he forced himself inside. Jack made his way through one of the three aisles, when a man with a long beard, jagged teeth and a cap covering the rest of his furry face, whispered, 'Hello Jack. I knew you would come. Don't ask any questions, just take this. Don't pay. Please, I insist. There'll be a bully at school. Put that thingy around his neck and then put the other thingy around your neck.'
'O-O-OK,' Jack stuttered and ran out of the shop.

Meanwhile, in the shop . . .

Ring ring, ring ring 'Hello?'
'There's another new kid coming your way. Sell him mistletoe.'
'Oh, right.'

So, this is my new school, thought Jack and in the playground there was a bully. Jack sneaked up and put the thingy around his neck. After three seconds, Jack felt dizzy and before he knew it, he was a fat, ugly bully.

Throughout that day, he made the bully say he was stupid and smells of manure and also made him kiss the teacher. Jack's real body acted the same as he usually did.

When Jack got home, he took the thingy off and everything was normal again, apart from the bully's life, that is.

Nicholas Merryweather (10)
Willerby Carr Lane Junior School